NOT OUT

NOT OUT

Dirk McLean

James Lorimer & Company Ltd., Publishers
Toronto

James Lorimer & Company Ltd., Publishers, acknowledges the support of
the Ontario Arts Council. We acknowledge the financial support of the
Government of Canada through the Canada Book Fund for our publishing
activities. We acknowledge the support of the Canada Council for the Arts,
which last year invested $24.3 million in writing and publishing throughout
Canada. We acknowledge the Government of Ontario through the Ontario
Media Development Corporation's Ontario Book Initiative.

The author makes a special thanks to the Ontario Arts Council's Writers'
Reserve Program for research and development of the manuscript.

Cover Image: Shutterstock

Library and Archives Canada Cataloguing in Publication

McLean, Dirk, 1956-
        Not out / Dirk McLean.

(Sports stories)
Issued also in electronic formats.
ISBN 978-1-4594-0176-1 (bound).--ISBN 978-1-4594-0175-4 (pbk.)

        I. Title. II. Series: Sports stories (Toronto, Ont.)

PS8575.L43N68 2012   jC813'.54   C2012-902777-4

James Lorimer & Company Ltd.,	Distributed in the United States by:
Publishers	Orca Book Publishers
317 Adelaide Street West, Suite 1002	P.O. Box 468
Toronto, ON, Canada	Custer, WA USA
M5V 1P9	98240-0468
www.lorimer.ca	

Printed and bound in
Manufactured by Friesens Corporation in Altona, Manitoba, Canada in
August 2012.
Job #77081

For my family: Renée, Jessica, Melissa,
and my mother, Jacqueline

CONTENTS

1 THE LEOPARD LEAPS TOO FAR

Whoooosh!

Dexter Armstrong almost lost his balance when he swung and missed.

"Strike one!" the umpire called.

Dexter's team, the Pelicans, was trailing the Raiders 3–0 in the eighth inning.

With runners on first and second, all Dexter needed was a base hit to load the bases and set things up for their lead scorer, Marco Leung, next at bat.

Dexter planted his feet in the earth, still damp from last night's early-April thundershowers. He squinted into the afternoon sun, then positioned himself with the bat held high, ready to send the ball to the moon. Or, at least, beyond the boundary into a row of tall evergreen trees.

The Raiders' aggressive pitcher, Spiros Pataki, zipped the ball to first base, but the Pelican runner got back to the bag with ease. Dexter held his position, waiting for Spiros's next pitch. When it came, it sailed low.

"Ball two!" the umpire called and gestured.

"Come on, Leopard, hammer it home!" Pelicans pitcher Harry Webster yelled from the bench.

Thwack!

Dexter knew the instant he heard the sound.

"Foul ball! Strike two!" the umpire called.

The ball had floated up and back, behind home plate. Dexter knew that he could not make another error. He had to come through for the team now. Otherwise, he would spend the rest of the season warming the bench. That much Coach MacGregor had hinted at. He trembled at the thought.

"Base hit, Dexter!" another teammate yelled.

Dexter was the Pelicans' only switch hitter. When he was in fine form, he could cause a pitcher to make error upon error — as well as hit home runs from both sides of the plate. But that was last year. With this season barely started, he had yet to find his groove. He switched to the other side of the plate, hitting left now, hoping to catch Spiros off guard.

Spiros's pitch was high. Very high. Dexter watched it sail above his head. He didn't even have to duck.

"Ball three!" the umpire called and gestured.

"Give us a hit, Dexter!" chanted some of the Pelicans.

Dexter felt the sweat beading on his face. A base hit, that was all he had to do. Or maybe Spiros would make another error.

Or maybe I can hit a home run.

"Use your big bat!" someone called.

The tension was getting to Dexter as he once again took his position. He wiped his forehead with his sleeve to prevent the sweat from getting into his eyes. Then he switched back to the right side. A calmness fell over him. He was feeling in the zone.

What happened next would linger in memories and be told from different angles for months to come — maybe even years — with heads shaken from side to side.

Spiros glared, wound up, and the ball shot from his hand like a rocket.

Dexter had no time to react. In fact, he would later recall that he barely saw the ball. It struck his upper arm. Dropping the bat, he grabbed his arm in pain.

The runners on first and second moved ahead as the Pelicans high-fived each other and yelled, "Bases loaded, bases loaded!"

But Dexter did not hear them. Instead of walking to first base as he should have, he bolted towards the pitcher's mound in a blind fury, not even hearing Spiros's apology, and dove into his chest, sending them both crashing to the ground. Dexter's fists connected with Spiros's head before he was pulled off by stunned teammates.

★★★

Suffolk Road Public School was both a junior and a middle school in Scarborough, a Toronto suburb. The students came from all sorts of ethnic backgrounds, with Asians being the slight majority. The school motto was *Care, Share, and Be Aware,* but the grade eights made up their own secret motto — *Dare, Swear, and Wear-whatever-you-want.* And they did.

Dexter, of African-Trinidadian heritage, was in grade eight. Average in height, he wore his wiry hair trimmed low. He had attended this school from kindergarten, and being on a team meant a lot to him. Especially a winning team. In the fall, it was cross-country. Winter was basketball. Spring was baseball — and baseball was his favourite. The Pelicans had a great win record and were considered a tough team to beat. Well, today they were being tested.

Dexter, thrown out of the game by the umpire, now stood on the edge of the field with his back to the school. Watching his team lose. Marco struck out, leaving the runners on first and second base. Then their pitcher, Harry Webster, fell apart, allowing three more runs for the Raiders in the ninth inning.

Could it get any worse? Dexter thought.

Yes, it could. The Raiders' closing pitcher struck out the top three Pelican batters in the lineup.

Bam! Bam! Bam!

At that moment Dexter dashed for the change room.

He quickly changed to his regular clothes and was just tying his shoelaces when his teammates sauntered in, kicking benches and swearing. Most avoided him.

"Coach wants to see you in his office, dirtbag," Marco Leung hissed.

Dexter ignored Marco, finished tying his shoelaces, and dumped his uniform in the hamper, except for his team cap, which wasn't dirty. He knew that Coach MacGregor did not like to be kept waiting.

"Nice dive, Armstrong," Randy, the centre fielder, called out sarcastically. "We could have used you on the swim team last winter."

"You cost us the game!" Marco Leung slammed his locker door.

Look who's talking, Dexter thought. *At least I didn't strike out. I just defended myself.*

But he knew they blamed him.

★★★

In the hallway Dexter took a fast drink at the cooler. He still had not decided exactly what he was going to say. *Maybe I should play the silent sorry role*, he thought. *Take the long speech from Coach and leave with my head hung down to my ankles.*

"Come in!" Coach MacGregor called when Dexter knocked. It sounded like he was speaking through clenched teeth. *Great.*

The walls of Coach MacGregor's office were crowded with framed certificates, plaques, and different incarnations of Pelican jerseys, all displaying the Pelicans' success. Dexter entered just as Coach hung up the phone, stood, and pointed to a chair. Dexter sat. Coach's face was red and he was frowning fiercely. Not a good sign. Dexter didn't wait for him to speak. He jumped right in with his own defence.

"Coach, that stupid Raiders pitcher had it in for me!"

"I don't think so, Dexter," the coach barked.

"He did! He hit me on purpose!" Dexter charged.

"You really expect me to believe that he hit you so you would walk and load the bases knowing that our slugger Marco was next?"

"But—"

"You played a switch-hitter's head game with him. You got him off his mark. All of that was tactically sound and it worked. He lost control of his pitching, hit you, and handed you a walk. You should've thanked him. But what did you do? You went ballistic like a bull-headed maniac. And we *might* have won with those bases loaded."

Coach MacGregor visibly sagged.

The wind went out of Dexter's sails too. "I'm sorry, Coach. It won't happen again," he mumbled.

"Look, Dexter, I know that you were a big part of the team winning the city championship last year.

Slugging homers, stealing bases by leaping like a leopard — adding speed from shortstop and third base, driving the ball into the gaps . . ." Coach MacGregor paused and looked Dexter square in the eyes.

"You have brought shame upon the team and your school. I can't tolerate that kind of behaviour. You're off the team. Turn in your uniform. You'll be lucky if Principal Gagnon doesn't suspend you."

Dexter was stunned. After what felt like forever, he stood up.

"My uniform's in the hamper," he whispered, holding back tears.

He took off his cap and placed it on the desk.

Suddenly he exploded, "It's always my fault!"

"You need to control your anger, young man," Coach MacGregor said coldly.

Dexter stormed out of the office, not even bothering to close the door.

A few minutes later, Dexter stood in front of the display case in the hall. It was filled with trophies, team photos, plaques, and ribbons.

I've seen pros get kicked out of a game for standing up for themselves when a pitcher hits them, he thought. *But not kicked off the team. It's just not fair.*

He stared at the trophy the Pelicans won last year. Remembering the joy.

What am I gonna do now? he thought.

2 NOT JUST A VASE

Dexter locked his bike in the basement of the apartment building where he'd lived with Aunt Nicole for the past two years — ever since his parents' accident. He bounded up the stairway to the fourth floor, jiggling keys on a Blue Jays key ring. Opening the door, he entered the two-bedroom apartment decorated with a mixture of Caribbean, African, and Asian carvings and batiks. It still looked like only his *aunt's* place, not *his* place. More like a museum, with all her stuff and a thousand rules. "Don't touch this. Pick that up. Straighten those hand towels." This was not his home. He'd never choose to live here. He felt rage boiling up inside him again.

Dexter took off his backpack and slammed it onto the coffee table in the living room, causing a tall oriental vase to fall onto the wooden floor and crack into two pieces. He took off his helmet and found himself using it to smash the two pieces into a hundred pieces.

Dexter was alone. Aunt Nicole had already left for her second job, which she had started at the beginning of the year. Part time, not far away. Her main job was accountant/bookkeeper for a large retail store.

Dexter washed his hands and opened the still-warm oven, removing his supper.

Then he had a flashback. One of hundreds in the past two years. *Mom and Dad lying in open caskets. Side by side. A car accident. A drunk driver.*

He released an agonized cry. *No more!*

He dug into the rice and pigeon peas pelau with chunks of pumpkin, along with baked tongue-scorching jerk chicken. He was ravenous.

"Chew your food properly before swallowing. We are not wolves," he remembered Aunt Nicole telling him.

He crammed his food into his mouth even more ravenously.

What am I gonna tell her about baseball? he thought.

The house phone rang and Dexter grabbed it.

"Yeah?" he answered rudely.

"Dexter, is that any way to answer a phone?" asked his aunt.

"Sorry, Aunt Nicole."

"I'm just checking to see that everything's okay."

"All fine. Thanks for supper."

"How was school? And your baseball game?" she asked. "One day soon I'll come to a game."

When cats learn to limbo, he thought.

"All fine, Aunt Nicole," he said, wanting to avoid further conversation.

"That's good to hear. See you in the morning, sweetie," she concluded.

Aunt Nicole would be home long before morning. Around ten tonight, to be precise. By then Dexter would be snoring in his room. His cell phone rang and he glanced at the display. His friend Atul.

"I heard you're gonna be a synchronized diver," Atul said, chuckling.

Dexter groaned. "Bad news travels fast." He dropped onto the plastic-covered sofa and swung his feet onto it. He would not dare do that if Aunt Nicole was home. She'd told him more than once that he should practice sitting "like a gentleman."

"Sorry, buddy. I know how much you love baseball."

Dexter didn't want to talk about what happened at the game, and he changed the subject. "How was your cricket match?"

Atul Dhillon was a real cricket buff. He not only played, but had an excellent memory for facts and trivia, especially regarding his ancestral team, India. He was Dexter's age, thirteen, and wore his shiny black hair in spikes.

"Cricket was as cricket always is — the best sport for body, brain, and spirit. However, buddy, my fast bowling is getting *better*."

"That means you guys lost," Dexter said wryly.

"The Morningside Breakers bat-tered us like a hur-ri-cane," Atul rapped.

"You mean swamped you like a tsu-na-mi."

"Thun-dered like a thun-der-storm."

"Mon-sooned like a monsoon," Dexter added.

They both cracked up. Dexter was relieved to have someone to be silly with. Especially after the terrible day he'd had. His friendship with Atul was an easy one, established just over a year ago when they'd met at an arcade and discovered they both liked hip hop and went to the same school.

"Wanna hang out Saturday morning?" Atul asked.

"How about Friday after school?"

"Nah, cricket practice."

"On a Friday afternoon? Coach Wickedson must be a monster."

"It's Coach Wilkinson."

"Coach Whatever."

"No, not Coach Whatever. Coach Wilkinson."

They both had another fit of laughter.

"Okay, Saturday. Later."

After Dexter clicked off, he picked up the pieces of the vase and placed them in a garbage bag by the door. Aunt Nicole, he knew, would not be pleased.

★★★

The following morning Dexter woke up to a tapping on his shoulder. He rubbed his eyes and opened them. At eye level was a garbage bag. The one that had been by the door.

Uh-oh, he thought, sitting up in bed.

"I can explain," he offered.

"I certainly hope so." His aunt folded her arms and glared at him.

"See, I came home and was taking off my backpack. I . . . I was too near the coffee table and . . . and it swung and knocked over the vase."

"I've told you a hundred times to take off your backpack with more care. By the door."

"Sorry, Aunt Nicole."

"Not as sorry as you will be. Dexter, I love you. You are my sister's only child. I promised her when I viewed her body in the casket that I would look after you, teach you what's right. Now you must learn that there are consequences to certain actions."

Here comes the sermon.

"You've recently turned thirteen. A teenager. So, whenever in the near future you get a part-time job, earning money, you will begin to pay for this vase. Two hundred and fifty dollars. Plus taxes."

"All that for just a vase?"

"Just a vase to *you*. I value the things I work hard for. And another thing, I don't believe your story. There are too many pieces in this bag for it to have been just knocked over. Next time, Dexter, tell me the truth."

Dexter didn't respond. He knew she'd moved closer to Suffolk Road PS so that he would not have to change schools. She probably regretted it by now.

"What could have made you so angry this time?" she wondered aloud as she walked out of his bedroom.

Dexter kept silent.

3 ENOUGH IS ENOUGH

As Dexter powered his bike to school, he suddenly re-membered something he had pushed into the back of his brain — Coach MacGregor saying that Principal Gagnon might suspend him.

This could be my last day at school ever, he thought. *I'll have to start a job on Monday to pay for the vase and my food and rent and . . .*

Be-beep! Be-beeeep!

Dexter looked up in time to brake from crashing into a shiny Volvo. Coach Wilkinson was pressing on his car horn.

There's that cricket coach who makes his players practice on a Friday afternoon, Dexter thought, watching the car ease into the staff parking lot. *Huh. He's too old to wear his hair in that straggly ponytail. Gotta be at least forty.*

★★★

Halfway through English class, Dexter was summoned

to Principal Gagnon's office as classmates snickered. He high-fived Atul on his way out. He didn't want anyone to know he was scared shitless. Yeah, the whole school knew the story. No doubt a dozen different versions of it.

The students thought of Ms. Gagnon as tough, but fair. Young for a principal, maybe late-thirties, she wore her dark hair long and curled and had a short, athletic build. She always wore splashes of colour with her usual suits, bright scarves or patterned blouses. Now Dexter sat in front of her.

"Dexter, I've read a report from Coach MacGregor. I know what it's like to play on a team and get angry when things happen that you don't think are right. Last year you had a few angry outbursts that were not called for — Mr. MacGregor reported them to me, and I saw you myself sometimes — but we knew you were dealing with the loss of your parents and so gave you a lot of slack."

She paused and leaned forward. "You must remember, Dexter, that when you play sports, you are not just representing your team but your school. You crossed the line yesterday by attacking the pitcher, but I am satisfied that your punishment of being removed from the baseball team is enough."

Dexter smirked.

"Wipe that look off your face! I have spoken with the principal at Brimley Road PS. He has assured me that the pitcher will not be pressing charges against you.

Now I will be informing your guardian of this incident and of my decision."

"Is that necessary, Ms. Gagnon?" he pleaded.

"Absolutely. Now back to class. This break from the team should give you some time to better your grades, which have fallen in the past couple of years. I do want you to graduate. I'll be keeping an eye on you, Dexter Armstrong." She got to her feet and ushered him out of her office.

Dexter dreaded Ms. Gagnon calling Aunt Nicole. Things with his aunt were bad enough already.

After school Dexter found an empty classroom where he completed most of his homework. The rest he would finish on Aunt Nicole's computer at home. He could not think of another way to stall so that he would arrive home after Aunt Nicole had already left for her evening job. He was supposed to be at baseball practice, after all.

Leaving school Dexter rode through U-shaped side streets. He carefully navigated the car-filled parking lot at Bamburgh Plaza. He locked his bike outside the Chinese supermarket, went inside to the bakery section, and bought one of his treasured snacks, an egg custard tart. *Dan ta*.

He passed the tiny Steeles Public Library with one hand on the handlebar while nibbling the *dan ta*. Food always made him feel better.

Dexter crossed Bamburgh Circle and entered Terry

Fox Park, where Canada geese fought for pieces of bread scattered by an elderly couple sitting on a bench. He continued weaving through a series of paved laneways between houses, careful to cross Birchmount Road at the traffic lights before pointing east towards Kennedy Road. He checked his watch and decided to head home at last.

Dexter let his backpack slide to the floor just inside the apartment door. Kicking off his shoes, he inhaled the aroma of steamed grouper cooked with tomatoes, onions, Spanish thyme, and a hot scotch bonnet pepper. He had to admit his aunt was a good cook. As he rounded the corner to the kitchen, he gasped. Sitting at the table reading a magazine was Aunt Nicole.

She wasn't supposed to still be here!

"Come, sit down." She pointed to the chair opposite to her.

Dexter sat.

"I'll bet you thought I was at work already."

Dexter remained silent.

"Answer me."

"Yes, Aunt Nicole."

"Well, you thought wrong. I took the evening off so we could have a little chat."

This morning a sermon, tonight a lecture.

"Don't even try to tell me you had a wonderful baseball practice. That 'All fine, Aunt Nicole.' Your principal called me." Her voice rose in pitch and

25

volume. She was angrier than he thought she'd be. "I'm tired, Dexter! Tired of working two jobs so you can have everything you need. Tired of you lying to me every chance you get. Tired of your outbursts."

She paused, and Dexter felt his resentment grow. She wasn't his mother! His mother was dead.

His aunt's voice softened. "Dexter, I know how devastated you were by your parents' deaths. I know how long it takes to get over that kind of loss, if in fact you can ever get over it." She paused again. "I understand why you're angry, but don't forget — I suffered their loss as much as you did. Delia was my only sister, and I can't tell you how many nights I cried into my pillow, how many times I asked God why . . ."

She's just trying to get my sympathy, Dexter thought. *Not gonna happen.* He watched as she straightened her back, then fixed him with a hard stare. "As you get older, Dexter, your anger could become a dangerous thing. And I have no intention of becoming afraid of a child in my own home. A teenager. I've seen enough mothers go through that. So enough is enough."

He stood up. "If you don't want me, I can call Social Services and they'll find a home for me," he boasted.

She didn't rise to the bait. "Sit down," she said calmly. "Yes, you could do that. But it wouldn't solve your problem. You would become an angry black teenager. Then an angry black man. And jails are full of angry black men."

Aunt Nicole slid a piece of paper towards Dexter. He picked it up, sat, and read:

Ozzie Clarke, Trombone Instructor
L'Amoreaux Community Centre

There was also a phone number and address.

"I stopped playing the trombone a couple of years ago when . . ." He didn't finish the sentence. "I hate the trombone!" He tossed the paper onto the table.

"Mr. Clarke remembers you as a promising student. He said three lessons a week and you'll sound like a pro in no time. Music is good to have in your life."

For the first time, Dexter noticed the instrument case on the floor beside her. She lifted it to a chair, opened it, and took out the trombone. "I've cleaned it for you. It looked so lonely and neglected."

Then sell it, for all I care, he wanted to say.

She took a breath and blew out. "Now either you go for trombone lessons after school or you find another sports team that will take you. I won't have you hanging around Pacific Mall after school like a vagrant."

They sat in silence for a moment.

"Go wash up and we'll have supper," she said.

Dexter rose from the chair and shuffled to the bathroom. He wanted to scream. Yet he didn't. He wanted to punch the walls. Instead he washed his hands. And his face — the water mingling with his tears.

4 THIS GAME IS CRAZY

Just before class, Dexter approached Atul at his locker.

"You look aw—" Atul started.

"Don't say it. I feel bad enough already," said Dexter. "I had trouble sleeping last night." Which was an understatement. He'd lain awake half the night mentally kicking himself for screwing up so royally, and the other half thinking how unfair the world, *his* world anyway, was.

Atul removed a red cricket ball from his locker and tossed it to Dexter, who caught it.

"See, you can catch it," Atul said. "Not so different from a baseball. And you don't even need a mitt."

"Meaning?"

Atul chuckled. "Dexter, sometimes you can be so slow. There's an opening on our squad. An 'alternate' position. You might get to play some games. You never know."

"What kind of game is cricket, anyway?" Dexter sneered. "It's never on TV."

"Sure it is. Okay, it costs more to get the channel, but the World Cup is always on it. Come on, just try out, Dexter," he pleaded.

"Look, Atul, I don't want to be part of a team nobody cares about. A loser team that's never won any championships." He tossed the ball back to Atul.

His friend looked crushed. He closed his locker, snapped the combination lock, and walked away.

I wish people would stop giving me advice, Dexter thought, scowling.

Throughout the day Dexter and Atul avoided each other as best they could. After lunch it started to rain. This meant that cricket practice would be indoors, Dexter knew.

He stood in the hall outside of the gym peering through the small rectangular glass panel in the door. Cricket practice was well underway. He had never really paid attention to this game before. He noticed that two boys holding bats stood at opposite ends of a straight line. There was a flat box with three short wooden poles sticking out of it behind each batter.

One batter stood in front of the box with the sticks, tapping the end of the bat on the floor as he waited for the ball, which Atul was going to pitch — no, *bowl* — to him. He knew that much. The other batter stood beyond Atul. Then Atul tossed the ball in the air, caught it, and took two steps, stopping at a line, all the while twisting his body and his arms like a contortionist before letting go of the ball. When he did, it bounced once before the batter swung the bat, slamming the ball to his left towards the wall.

"Hilarious," Dexter muttered.

He tried to imagine a baseball pitcher running from between second and third base to the top of the mound and firing a pitch that bounced once before the batter hit it. Crazy!

What he saw next was the first batter running with his bat towards the line from where Atul had delivered the toss, then touching the line with the end of his bat. At the same time the non-batting batter took off, passing the first batter going in the opposite direction and also touching his bat to the line.

Was that a run? Dexter scratched his head. He noticed with amusement that the bat was flat on one side, which made it easier to hit the ball. Still, the batter required the same hand-eye coordination a baseball batter had to have.

Three grade eight girls came up to the door. The tallest one tapped Dexter on the head and nudged him aside to look through the glass. She motioned to her companions and pushed open the door to the gym. Dexter decided to trail behind them. They all stood against the back wall quietly.

Atul looked over, grinned, and waved. After about fifteen minutes, the practice came to an end. Coach Wilkinson brought the squad, its members all from grades seven and eight, into a huddle for final instructions and a cheer. He did not bark orders. Maybe he wasn't so awful, after all.

Dexter suddenly missed the camaraderie of a team. But playing cricket after the glory of baseball? No way!

Atul crossed to Dexter.

"Ladies, this is my buddy Dexter." Obviously he'd forgiven Dexter for his mean words earlier. "Dexter, meet Yaeko, Mumbi, and Sonia." He winked at Sonia and she looked him up and down. She was the tall girl who'd tapped Dexter on the shoulder.

"Who are you winking at, Atul Dhillon?" she said, putting her hands on her hips. "You better not let my boyfriend catch you doing that."

The girl named Mumbi piped up with "She doesn't have a boyfriend!"

She and Yaeko laughed at Sonia.

"Yet!" Sonia boasted, undefeated.

She sauntered off towards the other cricket players, followed by Mumbi and Yaeko.

"Sonia likes you, Atul," Dexter teased.

"Maybe. I wish she was shorter. I'll have to stand on my toes to kiss her."

"See, you're talking about kissing already. Kiss her sitting down then, idiot," Dexter advised.

"Enough about me. What about you getting a girlfriend, a steady-steady?" Atul pointed towards Mumbi and Yaeko.

"Nah, my life's too complicated right now. I'm sorry about what I said to you about cricket."

"We're still on for Saturday?" Atul asked.

"Pacific Mall."

They touched fists.

Dexter watched Atul stride over to the girls and put his arm around Sonia's shoulders. She didn't move away.

The rain had stopped by the time Dexter left school. He began cycling for home. The more he thought about it, the more he dreaded ending grade eight without playing on a sports team. Taking trombone lessons again was his biggest nightmare. What about soccer? Yes! He had always turned down the soccer coach in favour of baseball. Perhaps soccer could be his salvation.

5 QUEST FOR AN OFFER

Bzzzzzzz!

Dexter opened his eyes, reached for the alarm clock, and shut it off. He lay in the semi-darkness hoping that Aunt Nicole hadn't heard it, or if she had, then told herself he still had some homework assignment to finish. He did not need yet another lecture. *Fifteen more minutes and she'll be gone*, he thought. Then he could carry out his plan.

Dexter rose from the bed and crept to the window beside his poster of baseball superstar Jose Bautista to see if it was raining outside, for that would ruin his plan. It was slowly getting light out and he could see no rain. All clear so far. Then he crawled back into bed and lay on his back, pulling the blanket up to his neck in case Aunt Nicole came in before she left. Sometimes she did that so she could remind him about some errand, like dropping off her dry cleaning. On those mornings he would mumble an okay and, to his surprise, remember everything upon waking an hour later.

Dexter looked at the clock. Six-o-four. *Man, this is a long fifteen minutes. I'd prefer a shorter fifteen minutes.*

He smiled at the way his brain operated. Finally it was six-fifteen. Dexter cracked open the door and listened. Silence. He walked along the darkened hallway, noticing that the lights were all off ahead in the living-room area and the foyer. *Yes! Coast was clear.*

He dressed in his track suit and trainers, and retrieved a basketball from his closet, then took the elevator down to the underground garage. At this time of day, the visitors' parking area was almost empty of cars — perfect for practice. He started moving the basketball, a heavy substitute for a soccer ball, between his feet while running from one end of the area to the other. Then he pretended that a player was chasing him. He stopped the ball suddenly with his heel, faked a pass, then passed it back to an invisible teammate.

He did this a few more times. At last he felt ready for the soccer coach to say, "All right, show me what you can do, my boy."

★★★

Dexter walked onto the soccer field at school. His trainers were getting wet from the overnight dew on the grass. The cloudless sky signalled the beginning of a perfect spring day. Ahead Coach Oyemanga was playing goalie while the striker, a kid on the soccer team, took penalty distance shots on him. After every shot — they all failed — the coach gave the striker some pointers. Dexter watched, hoping that he would have a turn to try to score on Coach Oyemanga, who was short, but fast. When the coach gave the striker an exercise of standing in front of the goal, tossing the ball in the air and heading the ball into different parts of the goal, Dexter saw his chance and approached Coach Oyemanga.

"You're pretty good, Coach," Dexter said. "You should play for Toronto FC."

"Dexter Armstrong." Coach Oyemanga shook his head. "I've heard about your troubles, my boy."

"Aw, Coach, that's all in the past. Today is a brand-new day. And I'm sure I can score on you," Dexter said.

Coach Oyemanga threw his head back and laughed, not in a mocking way, Dexter thought, but out of genuine amusement. Then he said, "In my village in Nigeria, a leopard once came and snatched a baby from his sleeping mother's arms. I see why they call you the Leopard. You are fearless."

"And because I *am* fearless, you are going to give me a spot on your amazing team!" Dexter proclaimed.

Coach Oyemanga looked at Dexter and again shook his head.

"Dexter Armstrong. Every year I came to you. I said, 'Come and join my soccer team.' And every year you chose baseball. I am truly sorry to say that all of my spots are taken. I wish you luck."

Dexter walked away, kicking at the grass in frustration. Then he began to smile because at least somebody wanted him. That gave him hope.

★★★

All morning Dexter tried to think of which coach to approach next. At lunchtime Dexter spotted the tennis coach, Mrs. Gangasingh, on duty in the cafeteria. Although he barely knew how to hold a tennis racquet, he approached her.

I must be getting desperate, he thought.

Mrs. Gangasingh, not much taller than Dexter, looked stronger than most of the male staff, with her muscular arms and calves.

"Mrs. Gangasingh, have you tried today's chicken tandoori?" he asked. "It's pretty good."

"I'm vegetarian," she stated and looked more closely at him. "Aren't you Dexter Armstrong?"

"In the flesh," he said, struggling to sound cheerful. She scowled, but Dexter pressed on. "Are you coaching boys' tennis along with the girls' team this spring?" he asked, already knowing the answer.

"Yes, I am," she said flatly. She peered at something behind Dexter with bird's-eye skill.

"Peter Chuang Tzu Chao, chew your food, don't wolf it down!" she shouted.

"And you have room on the boys' team for another

36

talented player," Dexter stated rather than asked.

"No."

"No? You won't even let me try out?" he asked. *Geez,* he thought. *Can't believe I have to beg to be on a team I don't really want to be on.*

"I don't coach people who fight," she said finally.

Dexter turned and walked away, struggling to keep his mounting anger in check. If anyone said anything to him now, he would explode, he was sure of it. He checked his watch. Fifteen minutes before lunch was over.

Maybe I can get Coach MacGregor to take me back, he thought, *if someone speaks on my behalf. Someone other than that badmouth Marco Leung.*

★★★

"Coach MacGregor made it very clear that he wanted you off the team, Dexter," the school principal said. "I cannot intervene. It's his decision. You're very determined and I admire you for that. Have you thought of cricket?"

Has Atul been talking to you? he wondered.

"Er . . . no . . ." he replied.

"Coach Wilkinson can be stubborn, but he's fair," she said. "As long as you can keep that temper of yours in check."

"Cricket? I'll . . . um, I'll talk to him," he said, forcing a smile.

Catching a ball without a mitt — how stupid is that?

After school Dexter went looking for Coach Wilkinson, but he was nowhere to be found. The office secretary said that he had left earlier, not feeling well.

"Geez, this coach sounds like a wimp," Dexter muttered to himself as he left the office. "Guess that's why he coaches cricket, not baseball."

6 A LITTLE LESSON

Saturday morning. The time for housework, laundry, and grocery shopping. Aunt Nicole had taught Dexter how to use the washing machine, which sat in the large kitchen with the dryer above it. She made him responsible for cleaning his own clothes, but she ironed some items so they'd look "proper," whatever that was.

Dexter glided the vacuum cleaner along the hallway. He had already completed the bedrooms. Aunt Nicole had mopped the kitchen floor and taken care of the bathroom. He dreaded the day the bathroom would be added to his duties. Yellow rubber gloves, sprays, rubbing, scrubbing on knees, *yuck!*

"I'm going to prepare you to be a self-sufficient man so you won't have to depend on a woman for your survival," she had said.

For the moment, he was indeed dependent on a woman — Aunt Nicole.

By ten the chores were done. Dexter showered, then dressed in laundered jeans, a t-shirt, and a Sean Jean sweatshirt, and strolled into the kitchen just as the oven timer went off. He opened the oven and, using an oven pad instead of Aunt Nicole's flowery oven mitts, removed a muffin pan of six steaming rye muffins topped with sunflower seeds. His dad used to make muffins for family breakfast on Saturdays. Now *he* did. It seemed right.

Dexter scrunched up his face and swallowed the spoonful of cod liver oil Aunt Nicole held out to him, followed by a quick gulp of guava juice. A forced weekend ritual. She no longer believed that he took the oil during the week.

Aunt Nicole had already prepared slices of bosc pears, scrambled eggs with tomatoes and red onions, plus a pot of roasted barley-flavoured Horlicks.

She bit into a muffin. "You've outdone yourself this time, Dexter," she said.

Dexter's response was a grunt, though he felt oddly pleased by the compliment.

"So are you ready to begin trombone lessons?"

His pleasure vanished. "I don't think I'll need those lessons," he said, scowling. Why did his aunt always do that? Follow words that made him feel good with words that made him feel bad?

"And why is that?"

"I'll be on a team by next week."

"What team?"

"I'm not sure yet . . . I'll let you know as soon as it's decided, Aunt Nicole."

"And who will be making the decision, you or a coach?"

Dexter wondered if Aunt Nicole was trying to trick him. He held up a finger to indicate that he was chewing, while searching for a reply. And while getting his temper under control.

"I will. I ... um ... I've had meetings with different coaches." He took a deep, calming breath. "These eggs are fantastic," he said, changing the subject. "I can even taste the nutmeg."

★★★

Pacific Mall was a monster of a mall, a few blocks from Dexter's home. It looked like an airport hangar from the outside. Inside were over two hundred bustling Asian shops offering clothing, jewellery, electronic gadgets, DVDs, medicinal herbs and teas, and exercise equipment — all high-end and mid-priced and located on the main floor. That is not what attracted Dexter and Atul. Not today. On the second floor were two food courts. The main reason for their bicycle trek was also tucked on the second floor — Playscape!

With the ten dollars Aunt Nicole gave Dexter as his weekly allowance, he used half and filled his playcard with credits. He and Atul bypassed the game where you timed dropping the small basketball into a hole for a slam winner. Both Dance Dance Revolution Extremes had lineups, so they headed straight to the super bikes, swiped their playcards for the one-credit race, and climbed aboard, side by side.

"Dubai or Thailand?" Dexter asked.

"Himalayas, man. I feel like going through the mountains today," Atul replied.

"And feel the breeze rushing through your perfect hair," Dexter joked.

"If you had my hair, you'd want that feeling also," Atul countered.

Indeed there was a fan above the motorbikes to create the sensation of wind. Engines selected, tires selected, and race number one began. They drove through mountains, past Tibetan temples, on rough terrain and paved roads, hitting speeds of 260 kilometres an hour with deafening sounds, performing acrobatic tricks leading to a one-two finish. Atul took the first round of seven, pumping his fists in the air like an Olympic champion. And the second round. Then Dexter's competitive nature kicked in and he won the next five races before they stopped. This was the feeling he had been missing this week, not being on a team.

If he was going to approach Coach Wilkinson on Monday, he would need to know something more about cricket. The Dance Dance Revolution Extremes, ever popular, still had lineups. He and Atul took a break and Dexter treated them to cold mango bubble teas with black tapioca balls floating like eyes in some weird science experiment.

"Hey, Atul," he said. "I was thinking I'd go see Coach Wilkinson on Monday."

Atul looked incredulous. "I'm sorry? The noise. Could you repeat that?" he asked.

"I said, on Monday I'm going —"

Atul burst out laughing.

"You heard me," Dexter said and punched Atul's arm. "So will you teach me some stuff about cricket?"

"Well, my boy, it will take twelve years of solid work if you're serious, for cricket is a serious sport for the serious-minded athlete," he said solemnly.

"Cut the crap, man. It's either cricket or a freakin' trombone. And I'd rather die than play that thing again."

Minutes later they raced their bikes to Atul's house on a horseshoe-shaped street on the west side of Terry Fox Park. It was now lunchtime, yet neither of them was hungry, despite the aromas that greeted them. Actually Dexter had smelled the familiar spices five houses away. They rushed in the side door of the spacious four-bedroom house with solar roof panels to the kitchen where Mrs. Dhillon was frying samosas.

"You guys are back early," she said.

"Hi, Mrs. Dhillon," said Dexter.

"I'm grabbing some gear to teach Dexter cricket," Atul said, heading to the basement.

Mrs. Dhillon glanced at Dexter while scooping out

a samosa from a pot of hot oil and placing it on a paper towel. "So you are going to learn cricket," she stated.

"I'll try," he said.

"There's no such thing as *try*. You either do something or you don't do it. I did not become a real estate mogul by saying I would try to sell some properties," she scolded, waving her finger at him.

He liked Mrs. Dhillon, but he kept hoping that Atul would hurry up. He was not in the mood for another lecture from a grown-up. He had had enough this week.

"You can be so serious, Dexter," she said with a smile. "I'm not a mogul. I said that to be funny."

Right, another jokester!

Mrs. Dhillon dropped some already cooled samosas into a brown bag. Then she pulled out four boxes of juice from the fridge, packed it all in a plastic bag, and handed it to Dexter, saying, "You athletes are going to need these."

"Thanks, Mrs. Dhillon," he said, accepting the package.

"Did I ever tell you that my grandfather played cricket for India?" she asked just as Atul ran breathless into the kitchen.

"Ready," he announced. "Dexter, my great-grandfather never played cricket for India. But he did go on a six-day hunger strike to end the war with Pakistan."

Dexter did not know who to believe. The Dhillons were such a house of exaggerators.

"I cannot even get you to fast for one day at Diwali," she complained. "Dexter, say hi to your auntie for me. And remember what I said."

He nodded. *No trying. Do.*

★★★

Dexter and Atul wheeled Atul's older brother's cricket kit through Terry Fox Park to the permanent cricket pitch between two soccer fields.

Dexter stood while Atul tied the pads onto the front of his legs — two straps below the knee and one above the ankle. He walked around feeling the new weight and bulk of the leg pads.

"Without these, a fast ball from a professional like me would shatter your knee," Atul said.

Atul spread plastic cones around to create a boundary, marking out the area of play. The cricket pitch was bumpy and worn. Atul explained the wicket as he pounded the three wooden posts, called stumps, into the earth at one end with a mallet and placed two sticks, or "bails," across the top of the stumps. He instructed Dexter to set another wicket at the opposite end of the pitch, about twenty metres away.

"This is the popping crease line," Atul said, drawing a line about a metre in front of the wicket. "As a batsman, you stand sideways on either side of the line like this and defend your wicket with your life." He demonstrated, tapping the end of the bat, the "toe," on the ground, just as Dexter had seen at the gym practice.

Next Atul showed Dexter how to grip the bat with the flat side forward for striking the ball. Now Dexter was ready. Atul stood at the opposite end and jogged a couple of steps, then bowled to Dexter. It was weird for Dexter to see someone running and throwing a ball at him, as opposed to standing in one spot and pitching. As the red ball bounced on the ground and rose to Dexter's chest, he stepped back towards the wicket, raised the bat, and accidentally knocked the wicket down before he could strike the ball.

"You just hit your own wicket. Out!" Atul called and raised his right hand with his forefinger pointed to the sky. "That's okay, we'll do it again."

Dexter quickly picked up the stumps and bails, re-assembled the wicket, and took up his position once more. Atul stepped back farther from the opposite crease, ran up faster, did a slight hop — Dexter learned later that this was his trademark — and bowled the ball, crashing it into the wicket before Dexter could even react.

"What the heck was that?" Dexter asked. "I thought you were teaching me how to bat."

"I am," Atul said as he walked towards Dexter. "I am also making you aware of different pitches, like a baseball coach would. The ball landed there." He pointed close to the wicket.

"I thought you were going to bowl it like the first time," Dexter said.

"Sorry. Anyhow, that second bowl is called a 'yorker,'" Atul continued. "No two bowls are exactly alike. You gotta watch the ball from the moment it leaves the bowler's hand till the moment you strike it with your bat, *and* keep watching where it goes as you run to the opposite crease line."

"Like running to first base?" asked Dexter.

"Well, sort of," said Atul. "Except that your non-batting partner, the batsman at the opposite wicket, will run down the pitch at the same time you do, but in the opposite direction, to score a single run or double."

Batsman, bowler, yorker, Dexter thought. "What else, Coach?"

"If you strike the ball — you're the striker — and it bounces before it reaches the boundary, where the cones are, and goes beyond it, that's an automatic four runs. Once you see that, you stop running and return to your crease line. If the ball goes past the boundary before touching the ground, it's like a grand slam — six runs automatically. And unlike baseball, you get to keep batting, racking up scores until you are 'caught out' or 'run out' or 'stumped.' Or . . . the game runs out of time and you are declared 'not out.'"

"So with my baseball training, I should be hitting a lot of sixes," Dexter said with a laugh.

"You'd better be. We need lots of sixes this season,"

Atul said. "First you need to get on the squad." Atul moved halfway down the pitch and bowled under- hand to Dexter, allowing him to get used to hitting the ball with different strokes to various parts of the field. "Good strokes, my worthy apprentice," Atul called out. "Let's take a break."

"My aunt, when she's not giving me grief, has some strange ways. She calls a break a 'segment of refresh- ment,'" said Dexter.

"It's her upbringing, that's all."

Dexter shook his head. "She could just say 'refresh- ment.'" He removed a box of pineapple-mango juice from the bag and tossed it high to Atul, who caught it with two hands and pulled it into his chest.

"See. That's how you'll field," he said.

"Right, no one-handed hijinks. I get it," Dexter replied.

Moving to the permanent metal stands for teams and spectators, Dexter and Atul devoured Mrs. Dhillon's samosas like starving piranhas.

"These leg pads are so big — how do you get used to them?" Dexter complained.

"It will take a while. At least they're not heavy," Atul replied. "In my great-grandfather's day, they weighed a ton, especially when it rained and they absorbed water."

"Imagine a baseball player with these on running to first base, then second . . ." Dexter shook his head as they walked back to the pitch.

Atul chuckled. "Sliding into third base and not being able to get up. I'm glad I don't have to wear them to bowl."

"You'd look silly," Dexter agreed.

"Now that you mention 'silly,' some of the fielding positions are called that," Atul said, and ran around in a circle to areas closest to the pitch, pointing with his bat. "Silly point. Silly mid-off. Short mid-wicket. Silly mid-on. Forward short leg. Short leg. Short square leg."

"That's silly!" Dexter cracked up.

"No, no, this last one's called short square leg. Silly's over there." Atul pointed.

They both collapsed on the grass in stitches. When the laughter subsided, Atul said, "One more funny thing about cricket. We say 'innings' just like in baseball, but in cricket we say 'innings' with an 's' even when we're talking about only one."

Dexter shook his head. This game was so weird.

Atul suggested they continue the practice. Dexter took up his batting stance. This time Atul moved back to his original position. He ran up to the popping crease and bowled down to Dexter with slow- and medium-paced balls — no yorkers or fancy spinners.

Sometimes Dexter hit the ball beyond the pitch with a ground stroke; other times he swung and missed the ball completely. At no time did he swipe a four or a six. Then, after being bowled out when the wicket was sent flying again, Dexter slammed the bat onto the grass and started to walk away. *This really is a stupid game,* he thought. He'd never get any good at it!

"Come on, Dexter," said Atul. "You're learning."

"Not fast enough. I keep missing."

"Everybody misses some balls."

Dexter stopped walking and turned to face Atul. "I'll make a fool of myself. Coach Wilkinson will think I'm a dud. I'm not gonna bother," he said. He knew he sounded like a little kid, whining and giving up because he wasn't able to do something new. But he didn't care.

Atul approached him, a wry expression on his face. "Well, maybe you've got a point. Just think. If you give up now, you'll go on to perform with your trombone in concert halls all over the world . . . wearing a penguin suit . . . for sixty or seventy years . . . and when you die, they'll place your trombone in your casket and then . . . then you'll have to play that trombone for eternity . . ."

He trailed off, and the pair stared at each other for a long while.

"What does your mom put in those samosas?" Dexter said at last. "Maybe you got more cardamom mixed in with the peas and potatoes than I did, so it affects your imagination."

"Actually you have to be Indian for the full effects of the spices to fill your skull and be absorbed by your grey matter," Atul responded, deadpan.

"Enough!" Dexter declared. "I'll go see Coach Wilkinson."

Two adult cricket squads arrived and claimed the pitch.

"Guyanese and Sri Lankans. Let's stay and see what we can learn," Atul said.

So they did.

7 THE ORIGINAL BAT

Monday morning. Dexter stood outside of Coach Wilkinson's office. He went over in his head Saturday's practice with Atul. And he tried to remember what he had observed from the match in the park between the Guyanese and the Sri Lankans. At the same time, he hoped that Coach Wilkinson was well again and would be coming to school.

Dexter spotted two of his former baseball team-mates down the hallway and moved away from the door. He did not want them, especially, to know what he was up to. He knew what they'd say, and he was in no mood for it. Suddenly Coach Wilkinson rounded the corner and brushed past him, looking healthy and energized. Dexter looked back to see if his former teammates were still there. They were gone. He ran back and caught Coach Wilkinson as he unlocked his office door and entered.

Dexter followed him in. "Good morning, Coach Wilkinson. Can I speak with you, please?"

"I'm very busy. What can I do for you?" he said, opening his briefcase and taking out a large notebook.

Dexter quickly scanned the tiny office. The walls were covered with cricket memorabilia and framed photos, including one of a young batsman. *Must be Wilkinson,* Dexter thought. There were other photos of him posed with what looked like professional cricketers.

"My name is Dexter Armstrong," he began.

"The kid nobody wants on their team," said Coach Wilkinson, without missing a beat.

Geez, Dexter thought. *The whole school knows about me. One flash of temper — I still think that pitcher was aiming for me! — and I'm branded as a troublemaker for life.* He sighed. *I don't stand a chance.*

Coach Wilkinson closed the notebook and looked at his watch. He opened a closet, removed a bag with red leather cricket balls, a yellow rubber ball, a bat, and leg pads. He tossed a pair of gloves to Dexter, who caught them.

"Put those on. Pick up that helmet and walk with me," the coach instructed.

Dexter, somewhat stunned, did as he was told.

In the hallway Dexter prayed that no one would see them. He put the helmet on, hoping he would see where he was going and not trip along the way.

"Cricket is a sport with zero tolerance for brawl-ing," said Coach Wilkinson, walking briskly. "Players respect each other. Even those from other schools."

They entered the gym and headed to the corner at one end where he pulled two floor-to-ceiling parallel nets from the wall, creating a sort of alcove.

Gymnasts were at the other end near a balance beam. Dexter recognized one of the girls Atul had introduced him to. Mum ... something. He couldn't remember her name, so he hoped she wouldn't recognize him.

"Cricket is fast growing in North America. It's not as big as baseball — not yet. However, Dexter, it's a sport of fair play, self-confidence, and commitment," Coach Wilkinson said. He checked his watch, looking around as if expecting someone.

"I know you can play third base and swing a baseball bat," he continued. "Go in the nets" — he gestured at the stands of nets, set up to act like a baseball batting cage, Dexter realized now — "and let's see what you can do with the *original* bat, a cricket bat."

Coach Wilkinson set up an indoor wicket between the nets. He tied the pads onto Dexter's legs. Dexter took his position in front of the wicket with his feet astride an imaginary popping crease line. Coach Wilkinson bowled the rubber ball to Dexter, who demonstrated his rough skills. This ball was easier to hit. Being indoors made it bounce better than the red leather cricket ball with the seam. He watched the ball like Atul had taught him.

Coach Wilkinson gave him instructions he was able to follow, making slight adjustments to the way he held the bat and the position of his feet. After about ten minutes, Coach Wilkinson stopped.

"Have you played before, Dexter?"

"I've never played a game of cricket in my life," said Dexter. That was the truth. Although he did not mention his lessons with Atul.

"You take to it like . . ." He hesitated.

". . . like a duck to water?" Dexter said.

"Yep. That's about right." Coach Wilkinson chuckled. "There are six weeks left in the season. If you promise me you'll keep your temper under control, you can join us as the alternate. And, who knows, you might get to play and have some fun," he concluded.

"Thanks, Coach Wilkinson, I won't let you down." Dexter beamed. He now had a new sports home. Maybe not the one he really wanted, but it still sure beat trombone lessons. He removed the helmet and gloves and sneaked a peek at the gymnasts. The girl he'd met was on the balance beam in her own world, never even noticing he was there. Just then Atul blasted into the gym.

"Atul Dhillon, you're late," Coach Wilkinson scolded, clearly in good spirits.

"Sorry, Coach, it won't happen again," he apologized, winking at Dexter. "I'm ready to be the best bowler of your entire career."

"Atul, meet Dexter Armstrong. He's joining us this afternoon. Dexter, meet Atul Dhillon, my best bowler, who still needs some pointers," said Coach Wilkinson.

They shook hands as if for the first time.

During lunchtime, Dexter phoned Aunt Nicole at work to tell her the good news. *Now she can stop hounding me about the trombone!* Dexter thought back to when he'd last played. He had been in the midst of a trombone lesson when his aunt had shown up and told him the news about his parents' accident. He'd never wanted to play the trombone since.

He was disappointed to only get her voice mail. She still considered texting rude. He left a message telling her that he would be having his first practice with the cricket squad and would be home late.

After school Dexter was introduced to the rest of the squad. The captain, Boyd Norwood, a kid whose family had moved here from Australia a couple of years ago, barely shook his hand. Boyd led them through a warm-up stretch and a jog around the boundary, marked by plastic cones.

While jogging, Dexter watched as Coach Wilkinson wheeled out a heavy mat and rolled it onto the low-cut grass to create the cricket pitch. This was the same area where the soccer team practiced — between the two goal posts and the extended field of the precious baseball diamond. Cricket was certainly the orphan sport at this school. Orphan. He knew how it felt.

"Communicators, I am always impressed when you score runs. It's one of the fun parts of cricket," Coach Wilkinson began as the squad drew around the pitch.

"Sometimes a single run can be turned into a double and a double into a triple, if the partners see that it's safe," he continued, smiling at them. "We're going to practice sliding. Doing this well will help you nail each run cleanly with speed and with confidence." Dexter knew that he could already slide into a base and stand up quickly, especially after stealing the base. *I'm gonna ace this part!* he thought.

Coach Wilkinson picked up a bat and, holding it with both hands, sped towards a wicket and slid the bat across the crease line with one hand while extending the other hand for balance. Recovering quickly, he lifted the bat and ran towards the opposite wicket, repeating the action. The squad applauded his skill.

"Okay, think speed and be confident and alert. Partner up," Coach Wilkinson ordered.

This was not the sliding Dexter had in mind. Wicket-keeper Dan Mewigwans, a First Nations kid, placed a heavy hand on Dexter's shoulder. A big guy, with piercing brown eyes and a ponytail, he towered over Dexter. Dexter looked up, grinned, and said, "I'm Indian, too. *West* Indian."

Dan deadpanned, "Shut up. I heard the *East* Indian one from Atul." He patted his girth. "Run slowly 'cause I'm not that fast for an Ojibwe."

The first partners, Prakash and Sifiso, the squad's opening batsmen, stood at either wicket holding their bats. On Coach Wilkinson's whistle, they both ran to the opposite wicket, slid the bat across the popping crease line, turned, and sped back to their original positions, completing the drill. Next were partners Atul and Boyd. Then Carlos and Benny. When it was Dexter and Dan's turn, Dexter was surprised to see Dan, despite his words, moving quite fast. Certainly faster than Dexter, who in the bulky leg pads had to struggle to keep up. *So much for acing.* On the return down the pitch, he heard laughter. Boyd was rolling on the grass clutching his gut, he was laughing so hard.

Dexter flushed with embarrassment. He wished the field would open up and swallow him.

"Lift your knees higher when you run, Dexter, so you won't waddle like a duck," Coach Wilkinson said with a smile. "Don't worry, we all started that way. And clearly some of us" — he scowled at Boyd — "need to remember that this is a gentleman's game."

Dexter looked over at Atul, who gave him a thumbs-up. He began to feel better.

★★★

When Dexter got home, he was bone-tired. His body ached from using muscles he didn't know existed. *Why did the rules say the batter and non-batter both had to run with the bat from wicket to wicket?* he wondered. *Why not have both drop the bats, run, then pick up the bat again after making the runs?*

The guys who'd made up these rules were dead, Dexter knew. Just like his parents. The thought lingered as Dexter washed his hands and opened the oven door to take out the dinner Aunt Nicole had left for him. The plate was barely warm. Sometimes he wished he could come home to a piping hot supper like he used to. But not in this home on a weeknight. Aunt Nicole refused to get a microwave oven. He sighed.

Dexter's mood improved when he lifted the lid from the plate and saw one of his favourite dishes. Sea bass slices with green bananas and callaloo — a mixture of spinach and okra blended into a spicy sauce.

Halfway through the meal, Aunt Nicole phoned. He thanked her, saying, "This food is delicious, Aunt Nicole." To his surprise, he found he actually wished she were here enjoying it with him, listening to him tell her about his day. His home life was so lonely! But he remembered her saying once, not long after his parents' accident, that sometimes all you can do is reach for a better feeling bit by bit. He didn't get it then. But maybe he was beginning to understand it now.

Suddenly he regretted his angry outbursts around her, his deafening silences. She didn't deserve those. "Will you be home soon?" he asked.

He could tell he'd surprised her, too. There was a pause before she said, "I shouldn't be too late. Hey, I'll take you out for a big supper soon."

Somewhere other than the Victorious Vegetarian Bistro,

he hoped. She called herself a part-time vegetarian, and that was her favourite restaurant. He didn't mind going to it once a year, not more.

Then she asked about his practice and he said it was all right. There was no way that he would mention the leg pads incident.

"As long as you're having fun. I used to play cricket as a girl in Trinidad. With an old tennis ball."

"I didn't know that," Dexter said, taken aback. He realized that there was so much he didn't know about her. Maybe he would start asking questions. He'd learn more about his parents, too. After all, she and his mom had been close.

"My cricket days were a long, long time ago," she said with a chuckle, then added, "Cricket, you know, has a long history of mind-boggling highs and head-shaking lows in West Indian culture."

Dexter tried to picture Aunt Nicole running with leg pads on. Children probably didn't need them anyway. Not with a harmless tennis ball. He also wondered what his dad would think about him playing cricket instead of baseball. His dad had been such a baseball fan. Dexter could remember going to Blue Jays games with him, and watching games on TV, his dad cheering a good hit or yelling at the umpire. They'd had so much fun, and now ... He swiped away the sudden tears that welled up in his eyes and finished his meal.

8 THE ALTERNATE OBSERVES

According to Atul, a match was played when each squad completed ten "overs." An over was when six good balls were bowled to batters. As the alternate, Dexter managed the kit cases from the pop-up, open-sided tent — each squad had one of these tents on match days.

At this match against the Donley Heights Googlies, a squad of mostly Jamaican Canadians, he watched and learned all he could, noting a different level of play from the adult squads he and Atul had seen last Saturday. The Googlies won the coin toss and chose to bat first. Dexter analyzed the batters' strengths and weaknesses. Some of them had a swagger in their walk towards the pitch. Others seemed to wait until the last possible moment before striking the ball. As if they couldn't care less what kind of ball was being bowled to them. And yet, somehow, they hit twos, fours, sixes — confounding Atul and the other bowlers and fielders on his squad. They hit strong "pull shots," where the ball is struck at waist level and sent far into the field, and nicely handled "bouncers," where the ball bounces at chest or head level.

Will I ever get that good? Dexter wondered.

The Googlies racked up 62 runs.

During the break Coach Wilkinson gathered the squad.

"Okay, guys, that was some decent fielding. We know they're a solid batting squad. However, their fielding is not as strong."

"They look tired already," Boyd remarked.

If that was tired, I'd hate to see them fully awake, Dexter thought.

Coach Wilkinson extended his hand. The squad followed his lead, one upon the other. Dexter saw that Boyd avoided his hand and waited for another squadmate to put his first. *What's his problem?*

"We've scored over sixty-one against them before," Coach said. "Let's give them our 'A' game and have some fun. Now take some deep breaths, close your eyes, and picture how you're going to bat."

The Communicators had another surprise. The fielding Googlies showed no signs of being tired. They caught impossible balls. Their bowling was solid. The Communicators managed a hard-earned 47 runs before they were "all out" and the match was over.

As Dexter started to pack up a kit case, Boyd approached.

"We brought six balls," Boyd snarled. "Make sure you don't lose any of them." He turned and walked off.

Dexter watched his retreating back, wanting to shout that he knew all the frickin' pieces in the kit case. Atul had overheard Boyd and joined Dexter in packing up their gear.

"What's with Boyd?" Dexter asked.

"He takes being captain too seriously. Thinks it will help him when he runs for prime minister. Next year."

Dexter laughed for the first time that afternoon.

"Well, he better smarten up. He doesn't know who he's messing with." Dexter raised a fist.

"Keep cool. Don't let him get to you," Atul advised.

"Easier said than done," Dexter muttered.

They stored the gear in the orange minibus. "Hey, Atul, I see that Sonia's friend, Mumbai, is into gymnastics and —"

"Mumbi. If you're interested in a girl, you gotta know how to pronounce her name," Atul scolded.

"I'm not interested in . . . Mumbi. I thought she was new here, that's all."

"She came from Vancouver in January. Her mother's Chinese-Jamaican and her father's from St. Vincent and the Grenadines."

"A mixed-up West Indian. Nice."

"I could hook you up through Sonia," Atul offered.

"Nah, cricket before girls," Dexter said quickly.

Dexter wondered what he would even say to Mumbi. They did not have any classes together. Still . . . he really liked her.

On the minibus back to school, Coach Wilkinson pulled out his notebook and talked to the team as a whole. He pointed out what they did well first. Then where they could improve. And how they could reduce fielding errors. He would meet individually with players on mornings before school started. He invited Dexter to come to as many of those practice sessions as possible.

I'll be there, thought Dexter. *You bet I will.*

9 THE FAMILY EATS OUT

The rest of the week flew by. Early Friday morning Dexter practiced different strokes by hitting a sponge ball tied to a string hanging from the soccer goalpost. Coach Wilkinson had taught Dexter this drill. Though he made many mistakes, he remained committed to improving. He then noticed that Coach Wilkinson had been standing near the school's building, watching him with his notebook opened. They waved to each other and Dexter continued the drill.

In the hallway afterward, Dexter had the pleasure of running into three of his former baseball teammates. They elbowed him rudely while passing.

"So you're on the *communications* team now," Marco sneered.

Before Dexter could tell him it was called a squad, Randy said, "I hear they bat with a ping-pong ball."

Dexter's heart pounded. He wanted to punch the sneers off their faces. He made a fist, then stopped himself, turned, and walked away. His new sport was

a *gentleman's game,* he recalled Coach Wilkinson saying. Besides, another incident like the one that got him
kicked off the baseball team would spoil his last chance
of being in sports.

After Friday's practice of fielding drills, Coach
Wilkinson called Dexter into his office. Dexter knew
that his fielding was better than his batting. He had
played both shortstop and third base in baseball and
thought he was okay that afternoon. Still, when he
walked in, his heart was thumping.

"Dexter, I appreciate all of your efforts with the
after-school and early-morning practices," Coach began.

Uh-oh, there's a "but" coming, Dexter thought.

"Are you cutting me, Coach?" he asked.

Coach Wilkinson shook his head. "Of course not."

Dexter breathed out, relieved.

"We've got five more games scheduled before the
playoffs for the big grade seven and eight tournament
day," Coach went on. "I'm selecting you to play in next
week's match. At number seven." Coach Wilkinson
smiled and wrote in his notebook.

"Really? Wow." Dexter beamed. He wanted to ask
why number seven, not number two as an opener, or
number nine, ten, or eleven. All he managed to say was,
"I won't let you down, Coach."

"I like your commitment, Dexter," Coach said.
"And with your baseball background, you'll be able to
hit fours and sixes. You'll field at square leg. That's just

beyond third base in baseball." He handed Dexter a bat and a rubber ball. "Take care of this equipment while you practice this weekend."

Dexter thanked Coach Wilkinson and zoomed off with the gear to tell Atul his news.

★★★

Dexter was both excited and nervous, for he saw the upcoming match as a major test of his abilities. At Terry Fox Park that Saturday for practice with Atul, Dexter was anxious to start batting after setting up the gear. Somehow he made himself stay patient as Atul went over some of the finer points of fielding, like calling out your own name when a ball is sent high into the field instead of shouting "I got it" or "It's mine." That would better avoid a collision by two or three fielders.

"Bend on one knee and let a speeding ground ball come to you and scoop it up with both hands before throwing it to the wicket-keeper right away. Okay, time for a segment of refreshment." Atul laughed at his joke.

They savoured Dexter's first-time pumpkin muffins, canned coconut water, and *dan tas* he picked up from the Chinese bakery, along with Mrs. Dhillon's samosas and pakoras.

"Hey, Dexter, how come you bake muffins? You're the only guy I know who does anything like that . . . well, not counting my uncle Danny, but he has a restaurant."

Dexter answered between mouthfuls of muffin. "I dunno. My dad used to do some baking, and now I do. I just . . . like it."

Atul nodded and said, "Cool."

Now Dexter had a burning query, and not about food. "With cricket, everyone gets to bat until they're all out or the game is over. In baseball, the higher up you are in the batting order, the more times you get to bat. Why do you think Coach Wilkinson is starting me at number seven?"

"After the seventh batter, we three bowlers and Dan, the wicket-keeper, get to bat. We're called the 'lower order,' or the 'tailers.'"

"Sort of like some National League American baseball pitchers who don't bat so well, 'cause they spend most of their practice time pitching, right?"

"Yeah, but if our squad batting second has scored enough runs, the tailers won't need to bat," said Atul. "And that's okay, 'cause we could be tired from all the bowling in the first half of the match."

"So I could be batting last. I may not get to bat at all," Dexter said, dejected.

"No, no. One and two, openers. Three and four complete the 'upper order.' Five, six, and seven, the 'middle order.' You'll definitely get to bat. You'll be fine. I hope," Atul teased.

"Are you out to help me or scare me?"

"Be scared, Dexter, and tremble, for Atul Dhillon bowls like a thunderstorm in August."

"It's only April . . . you can't be that dangerous now," Dexter challenged.

"When I bowl, it's always August. Go to your wicket and defend it like a . . ."

". . . a gladiator!" Dexter declared.

"Wow . . . okay . . . I like that," said Atul, accepting the challenge.

Dexter, with much ceremony, donned the helmet and gloves, picked up the bat, and swung it left and right as if it was a sword, before settling at the crease with life-and-death determination. True, he was no longer a baseball leopard. He was a cricket gladiator trainee!

Atul showed no mercy. He delivered an arsenal of balls. This time Dexter was not frustrated even though he was stumped out, missed a lot of balls, hit a couple of fours, and just managed to touch the balls in other moments. He saw it as a necessary exercise, remembering his baseball coach saying that it was better to make all the mistakes in practice than on a game day.

He bit his lower lip in grim determination. He'd get this new sport or die trying.

★★★

Match day. Overcast. Cool. The Communicators versus the Flyers. They had lost to them a few weeks ago and wanted to win badly. Captain Boyd lost the coin toss and the Communicators batted first. At number three in the lineup, Boyd scored 24 blistering runs before he was caught out. Sugith at number five was run out on a first ball.

When it was Dexter's turn at number seven, he felt nervous. He had observed the Flyers' bowlers and they seemed as skilled as Atul.

Dexter hoped that he would remember Coach Wilkinson's training. See the ball early, be quick on your feet, be quick with the bat. And don't make a fool of yourself. The first ball was wide. He remembered not to go for it. One extra run in his favour. His first. Next he hit a couple of singles, which had him sprinting down the pitch and sliding the bat across the crease line.

"Come on, Dexter!" the Communicators cheered.

He grinned, refocused, and hit a pull shot for six runs. It felt like a home run — which is what a pull shot is in cricket. Except that the batter keeps on batting. He did not get to relax in the squad tent (the dugout in baseball). More singles. A four. After a total of 14 runs, the unthinkable happened.

Dexter had stepped forward to play a shot, realized that the ball was going wide, and let it pass untouched. The ball was caught by the Flyers' wicket-keeper. Dexter was still loitering outside of the crease line when the wicket-keeper hit the bails with the ball, causing Dexter to be "stumped."

The umpire raised his arm with the index finger pointing up.

Dexter was confused until the umpire gently explained it to him. Then he slumped off the pitch towards Coach Wilkinson and his squad-mates, who congratulated him on his fine batting. All except Boyd, who had not managed any sixes — only singles and fours.

"Your being stumped could cost us the match, orphan boy," Boyd said too softly for anyone else to hear. "You better remember how to field." His tone was menacing, and Dexter felt himself tense.

Atul scored 11. The other bowlers were bowled out. The Communicators had racked up a total of 72. The magic number was 73, the "target" for the Flyers.

The Communicators, led by Atul's skilful bowling, held the Flyers to 65. Victory! They had broken the losing streak at an important time in the season.

There's excitement in this game, after all, Dexter thought.

★★★

Next morning, Dexter was disappointed when the win got only a brief mention over the PA system.

"Yesterday the Communicators won their cricket match," a toneless voice said.

That was all. Nothing about it being an upset over one of the top cricket squads. Surely, the score was worthy of a mention.

Coach Wilkinson informed Dexter that he was now on the roster, replacing Ryan, a grade seven batter who wasn't performing too well. *Oh no,* thought Dexter. *I'm the new kid on the team and Ryan'll hate me for this, and maybe the rest of the squad will, too.* But then Coach Wilkinson told Dexter that he had already spoken with Ryan and the kid was okay with being the alternate and would still gain experience towards the next year. Dexter felt better instantly.

After he left the office, Dexter got to thinking about how for every practice, Coach Wilkinson had to wheel the huge mat to create their pitch outside. He had also heard him complain about the lack of a permanent pitch at Suffolk Road PS; it meant the squad always had to travel to other schools to play, or to the grounds of a league cricket club. They could never invite a squad to their home pitch, because they didn't have one!

If we did, we would have the same respect as the baseball team, Dexter thought.

Principal Gagnon stopped Dexter in the hallway. "Congratulations, Dexter, I see your cricket team is improving," she said warmly.

"The *squad* has been working hard, Ms. Gagnon," he replied, correcting her. Still it seemed to Dexter that she did not register the correct term. Squad. Baseball was her baby.

"So, you're fitting in well?" she asked.

"Uh, yes," he said.

The captain doesn't like me being on the team for some reason, but you don't need to hear that, he thought. Then he saw an opportunity. He grabbed it.

"Ms. Gagnon, wouldn't it be nice if the cricket squad had a permanent pitch out in the field? Something small ... simple ... not in the way of the other teams?" he said casually.

"Ah, yes, I see," she said, studying Dexter. "Unfortunately that's not in the school's plans or budget. Enjoy your day, Dexter Armstrong."

"You, too," he said cheerfully before heading off to class.

★★★

Harvest Moon Restaurant, in the heart of Scarborough, had a red roof with a slate gray exterior and two giant marble lion statues to greet you at the entrance, and an all-you-can-eat buffet of authentic Chinese dishes. Parking on a Saturday evening, its busiest time, was a challenge, but Dexter was happy that his aunt's choice hadn't been the Victorious Vegetarian Bistro.

It was a special occasion. Aunt Nicole had insisted they go out to celebrate Dexter's playing his first match in a new sport. She wore a pink-and-black flowered dress and her bright weekend lipstick, and smelled of lavender. Dexter was decked out in his best, too — light wool pants and a yellow button-down shirt under a plaid V-necked sweater.

The buffet had at least fifty mouth-watering items, and Dexter dug into his first plateful with relish. His aunt was a little more ladylike, using chopsticks as if she had done it her whole life. When Dexter was on his second helping, Aunt Nicole brought up a new subject.

"My father, your grandfather, hasn't been well lately," she said.

"Why didn't you tell me about Grandpa before?" Dexter asked. His grandfather still lived in Trinidad. Dexter's voice had an edge. "You don't have to hide stuff from me. Remember, I'm a teenager now."

"I didn't want to burden you, Dexter. You've been occupied with so many things — homework assignments, cricket, selecting a high school for the fall ..."

Dexter put down his fork. "He's not gonna die, too, is he?"

"No, no," she said quickly. "A touch of pneumonia is all."

"I've only met him once, when I was one year old. I can't remember what we talked about. He did most of the talking," Dexter deadpanned.

Aunt Nicole chuckled. "See, now, that is who you got your humour from. Skipped a generation, I always said."

Dexter cleaned his plate and returned to the buffet. He was just helping himself to a blackened Atlantic salmon steak when he heard a burst of laughter from a group of people at a big round table. Looking over,

Dexter spotted Boyd, seated with what must have been his family — brother, sister, mother, and father. A real family enjoying themselves.

Dexter's chest tightened. He felt a mixture of anger and envy he could not explain. He realized he missed sitting at a table with his mom and dad. Boyd caught his eye and Dexter watched his expression go cold. Dexter returned the expression, but when he sat down at his table again, he wasn't himself.

"Are you feeling all right, Dexter?" his aunt asked.

"Yeah," he mumbled. "We should do this more often."

"Okay. I'll work on it."

That night, as Dexter lay in bed, he thought about his aunt and all the things she'd done for him. It dawned on him that she was trying so hard to be both mother and father to him, and how did he pay her back? By smashing her favourite vase, and other acts of anger over the past two years. He began to realize that the anger started soon after his mom and dad died. Here he was in this life without a happy family like Boyd's. Just his aunt. And an ailing grandfather in Trinidad.

Then he thought more about his aunt. What was she to him? A lot, he decided. She looked after him as best she could, even taking a second job. Made sure he had nourishing meals every day, clean clothes. Took him out for a great dinner tonight. Maybe he *could* be happy with just her. Maybe it wasn't quite like having two parents, but hey, there were lots of kids in school who had only one parent. And maybe they were worse off than him, because at least his parents hadn't *chosen* to go away as some of theirs had . . . At last he drifted off, dreaming of brighter days ahead.

10 IN THE NETS

A drizzle of Monday morning rain caused Dexter to change his plans. He had wanted to practice outside — throwing the red leather ball high and catching it with both hands. He knew that the squad's main challenge when they fielded first was limiting the opponent's runs. It felt funny seeing a ball coming towards him and not having a glove for the ball to sink into.

As Dexter finished setting up the nets, Coach Wilkinson arrived with the three bowlers, including Atul, and they greeted each other with slaps on the back.

"Dexter, tomorrow's match is going to be a tough one," Coach said. "We haven't beaten the Spinners this season. We never beat them all of last season, either."

"Coach, tomorrow's a new day," said Dexter.

"Good attitude. As much as I stress playing well and having fun over winning, I'd like us to win this one."

The bowlers cheered.

"This little exercise is for you, Dexter," Coach

continued. "Remember, see the ball early. Be quick with the bat."

Dexter suited up and took his position at the crease. Coach Wilkinson nodded to the first bowler, Atul. Just before each bowler bowled, he called out the type of bowl for Dexter to mentally prepare for it. Then Dexter played the throw and repeated aloud the type of bowl it was. Then more bowling, now without calling out the type.

Just as Dexter was leaving, dripping with sweat from head to toe, Mumbi entered the gym. She stopped and smiled at him. He did the same, tongue-tied. They stood only inches apart. And just then, as luck would have it, Boyd entered the gym and squeezed between them.

"Don't stare at her like you're afraid of her," Boyd said. "Talk, orphan boy. *Muummbi* might bite, but that's okay."

"Get lost, Boyd," she hissed.

Boyd pretended she'd slapped him, holding his cheek.

"Ouch! Does she slap you around like that, too, orphan boy?"

"Mind your own business, Boyd," Dexter warned.

"That's *Captain* to you. And what you gonna do, attack me like you did that baseball pitcher?" Boyd challenged.

Dexter stared at him.

"I didn't think so. But I kinda hoped you would," Boyd said, and walked away.

"I gotta go practice," Mumbi said. She seemed embarrassed, but so was he.

"Have a good one," he said and flew towards the dressing room.

★★★

"'Have a good one'?" Atul said in disbelief. "So lame, Dexter. You need some lessons with girls, too."

"I don't have time for her. I mean . . . I'm not interested in her," Dexter lied.

They were walking towards homeroom.

"I would have complimented her instead," Atul went on. "Like 'Don't get too hot on that balance beam, you're already hot, baby. So hot, you're sending a laser beam of love to my heart. And every time we part, I feel it's gonna break in two, girl.' Something like that."

Dexter rolled his eyes. "Is that how you hooked up with Sonia?"

"Nah, all I did was whisper her name and she was mine," he boasted.

"Yeah, sure," said Dexter as they entered the classroom.

★★★

The next day the Communicators and the Spinners settled into their own pop-up tent with open sides.

The Communicators batted first. Their bowlers were exceptional, retiring most of the Communicators with ease. Boyd at number three squeezed out 25. When it was Dexter's turn, he seemed to bat forever. He managed singles, a double, and was awarded some "extras," totalling 21. No fours or sixes. Communicators: 66.

During the changeover, the Communicators gathered in their tent.

"Last time the Spinners scored 90," Atul said. "I say we bowl them differently or we're toast."

"What do you have in mind, Atul?" Coach Wilkinson asked.

"Slow balls, spinners, yorkers. No fast balls or bouncers," Atul replied, smirking.

"Fast balls are always expected when a squad thinks the opposition is desperate," said Coach Wilkinson.

Dexter recalled Atul telling him that bouncers were bowled to bounce at chest or head level. Experienced batsmen could read them easily, and some could hit pull shots for fours and sixes. If a bouncer struck a batsman in the head, a run was awarded to him. Too many intentional bouncers and the umpire could dismiss a bowler from a match.

"Good plan, Atul," said Boyd.

Coach Wilkinson looked at the squad. "Any questions?"

They shook their heads.

"So, guys, be prepared to sprint and cover all the

areas like silly mid-on, silly mid-off, short mid-wicket, short leg, and silly point in a heartbeat," Boyd instructed.

Not for the first time, Dexter had to suppress a fit of laughter hearing the word "silly."

"Dexter," Boyd said, "you're usually at square leg, so start at deep square leg and move up to square leg and short square leg when you have to." Boyd delivered the instructions like a challenge.

These positions were just left of the batter. Like covering third base in baseball. It was fine with him. The Communicators followed Boyd's instructions, limiting the Spinners to many singles. By the end of the overs, the score was even. The umpire declared the match a draw.

The Communicators celebrated like it was their victory before lining up to shake hands with the Spinners.

"Good plan, guys, well executed," Coach Wilkinson beamed. "Next week we play the Breakers."

"Oh no," Sifiso groaned. "They beat us before."

"They're even stronger than the Spinners," said Dan. "Powerful bowlers, too."

"Guys, guys," Boyd interjected. "Every team can be beaten on any day, my dad says."

"I believe that also," said Coach Wilkinson. "It's a week away. We practice, prepare, and do our best to beat the crap out of them!"

Wow! The squad looked at Coach Wilkinson with mouths opened. They had rarely seen him so fired up. And Dexter couldn't believe how much he was liking a game he'd once thought was for wimps. He headed for the bus gleefully.

★★★

All that week the squad practiced harder and with new purpose. They were focused on winning. Winning would be more fun than merely playing. Through it all, Boyd called Dexter various names — has-been, reject, and his favourite, orphan boy — when no one was within earshot.

How can I shut him up? Dexter wondered.

On Saturday Aunt Nicole informed Dexter that she had given notice for her part-time job and was quitting it the following week.

"I thought you needed extra money," he said.

"I needed to create a cushion, along with my investments, and I've done that."

"So we won't be poor, right?" Dexter asked, eyes fearful. "I don't want us to end up poor or the Children's Aid Society will take me away like they did Simon who lived on Birchmount . . ."

"No one is taking you away, Dexter."

"You sure?"

"Cross my heart and —" She stopped. "I'm sure. Let's have some breakfast."

I hope she comes to my matches, he thought. *That would be nice.*

Atul had scheduled a shorter-than-usual practice at Terry Fox Park because he was going to a Bollywood matinee with Sonia. He and Dexter had seen Bollywood movies and other movies together before. Today was more of a date movie. Sonia had offered to invite Mumbi if Dexter would go. Dexter had felt anxious and nixed that idea. Then Sonia asked Mumbi anyway, but she was not available. Dexter felt relieved.

Atul had bowled to Dexter for half an hour. He stopped and silently walked the length of the pitch, took the bat from Dexter's hand, and tossed the ball to him. He gestured for Dexter to go towards the other end.

"I can't bowl," Dexter said, taking up the position beyond the pitch.

"Fake it."

Dexter shook his head, ran up, did a little hop, and brought his arm around and tossed the ball down the pitch. It weakened as it reached Atul, who easily swatted it back towards Dexter.

"That felt awkward," Dexter claimed.

"Keep going. Forget about the hop — that's just what *I* do."

And he did keep going, for about fifteen minutes, becoming more comfortable. At last they stopped.

"I'm not suggesting you begin bowling as well," Atul said. "I wanted you to have the experience so you could read bowlers a little better."

"Neat. Are you heading for coachdom?"

"No chance. I want to make the Under-Nineteen national squad by the time I'm sixteen."

"You never said that before."

"Dexter, we never talked cricket before last month."

"I wish you luck," he said, high-fiving his friend.

"Your batting's improving," Atul said, dismantling the wicket.

"Yeah, but it's not exceptional. First eighteen runs. Twenty-one runs last week with no fours or sixes."

"Hey, I don't even average fifteen when I bat. Only Boyd is exceptional. He hits in the twenties and thirties."

"Yeah, well, he still seems to have a problem with me. Any idea why?" Dexter asked while packing the kit case.

"Dunno, but like I said before, don't let it get to you. It's not because you're black, 'cause Sifiso's his best buddy and he's black, too. Maybe he's jealous of you."

"Yeah, right," said Dexter. Not likely. Well, he'd just have to find a way to ignore Boyd and his taunts. "Enjoy your movie."

"I intend to."

They went their separate ways.

Tuesday came. Rain. Rain all week. The heavyweight match of the Communicators versus the Breakers was washed out. It would not be rescheduled. Salvation from defeat? No one would ever know. Dexter checked the schedule. The Stumpers. Another chance to prove that he belonged on the team.

11 MOTHER'S DAY

Dexter stood at the crease ready to bat. He looked down and saw that he was holding a baseball bat instead of a cricket bat. He heard laughter and knew that it was directed towards him. He turned and saw them: squad-mates, former baseball teammates, coaches, Principal Gagnon. Boyd Norwood. African drums beat rapidly. Then he saw his parents. He dropped the bat and ran to them. They gestured that he should go back. He tried to protest, then turned and walked back to the crease. Picking up the baseball bat, he suddenly realized that he was holding a cricket bat and a red ball was thundering down the pitch towards him as . . .

He woke up in a sweat, looked at the clock: 4:00 a.m. He groaned, rolled over, and managed to snatch another couple hours of sleep.

The spring mornings were getting brighter earlier. Warm air and the sight and scent of small gardens in full bloom greeted Dexter as he pedalled to practice, humming a soca tune.

Minutes later Dexter stood in the nets. The batting tee was positioned in front of him. He tapped the toe of the bat onto the crease, looked up, and imagined the bowler running up to his crease and then watched the ball float towards him and bounce up. He took a step backwards, leaned slightly and ... *THWACK!* The ball sailed towards his left, up, up.

★★★

At the Stumpers' match later that day, Dexter quickly reacted to a bouncer. Just like in the nets, he took a step backwards, leaned slightly, and ... *THWACK!* The ball sailed towards his left, up, up, and over the boundary at the Stumpers' field for six!

The Communicators' tent erupted, including Aunt Nicole, Sonia, Mrs. Dhillon, and some parents. Jubilation. Dexter's squad-mates surrounded him, congratulating him. Even Boyd did, but Dexter could tell he did it grudgingly. Oh well, maybe he was making progress. He had scored 20 to Boyd's 26 and it was enough to edge the Stumpers — *stump* the Stumpers — by four wickets. Meaning that the three bowlers, Atul, Carlos, and Benny, and Dan the wicket-keeper did not need to bat. Final score: 58–53.

★★★

Dexter placed two small bowls of fresh garden salad on the kitchen table while Aunt Nicole unwrapped their take-out rotis at the counter. She took a pair of dinner plates from the cupboard.

"I'm glad you came today, Aunt Nicole."

"Me too. I'd forgotten how exciting cricket could be."

This was the first time he had family watch him play a sport in two years. He hoped that she would come watch a game again.

"You brought us luck," he said, pouring tea into their mugs. He was happy to share supper with her after so many evenings alone.

"Oh, you and your squad would have won anyhow. You've learned to play well in such a short time."

"I didn't reach the goal that Coach and I set for the match. I only got twenty runs instead of twenty-five."

"You still won. Besides, if you had continued batting, I'm sure you'd have made twenty-five. Perhaps more." She placed thick slices of currant roll on two dessert plates.

"You really think so?" he asked, sitting down. The praise felt good.

His aunt nodded. "Your mom and dad, God rest their souls, would have been proud to see you play today."

Aunt Nicole sat opposite him and unfolded her napkin, laying it on her lap. Dexter dropped his chin, hiding the tears that welled up in his eyes. Both were silent.

"The anniversary is coming up soon," she said after a while.

"Yeah," he said. He picked up his chicken roti with his hand while Aunt Nicole cut into her vegetarian roti with her knife and fork. He took a bite. Then another. He'd be okay.

★★★

The morning announcement of the Communicators' win was delivered with more enthusiasm. It included the score and named their opponent. This was no accident. Dexter's plan had worked. Without telling anyone, not even Atul in case he tried to talk him out of it, he had designed a flyer and posted it on the office door and on the Announcements Table earlier that morning.

CRICKET
Suffolk Road Communicators
stumped
Pharmacy North Stumpers
58–53

At lunchtime in the cafeteria, Marco, Randy, and Harry approached Dexter while he sat eating alone and reading a novel for English class. Marco shoved a cell phone into Dexter's face like a microphone. Harry pretended he was shouldering a news camera.

"Dexter Armstrong, new cricket batsman extraordinaire, how does it feel to wear pads?" Randy asked. He drawled the word "pads" so it came out in two syllables.

All three guffawed.

"Do they give you all-day and all-night protection?" Marco asked.

Dexter picked up his glass of juice ready to throw it at them. Then thinking better of it, he put the glass down and loudly declared, "Sorry, gentlemen of invisible TV, I won't be giving any interviews today." And he made a show of returning to his novel.

A few students, including Mumbi, Sonia, and Yaeko, applauded Dexter. He smiled — mainly at Mumbi.

★★★

Dexter visited Ms. Gagnon and asked her again to build a permanent cricket pitch on the field.

"As I said to you before, Dexter, Suffolk Road PS is not committed to a cricket pitch. The 'squad,' as you corrected me the last time, seems to be doing quite well without one."

"True," Dexter admitted. "We won our last game."

The principal shook her head. "I'm sorry. But as I've told Coach Wilkinson every year, there's not enough interest to justify the expense." She spoke with finality. *Not enough interest, eh?* Dexter thought. *We'll see.*

***

Dexter and Atul met and hatched a plan. For it to work, the Communicators would have to win the next game and get through the playoffs. The Exciters, although not a dominant squad, were on a winning streak lately. They'd just beaten the Breakers, the team the Communicators would have played last week if the game had not been rained out.

Dexter and Atul finished their Saturday practice, dropped the gear off at Atul's house, and rode furiously to Pacific Mall. They hadn't been there in over a month, as both had been consumed with cricket fever. At Playscape they jumped on the super bikes and raced through Dubai. This time Atul was the winner of their five-race challenge.

Then he said, "Dexter, I'm lousy at picking out cards. Will you help me get a Mother's Day one for my mom?"

Something inside Dexter went bump. But then he said breezily, "Sure thing. We'll have to hurry. The mall's closing soon."

They rushed down to the main floor and entered the crowded greeting card store. With barely half an hour left before closing, the last-minute Mother's Day shoppers were mostly guys. Last year Dexter and Aunt

Nicole had pretended Mother's Day did not exist.

"What about this one?" Atul asked, handing Dexter a card.

Dexter read it and dropped it back in the rack, saying, "That's the kind of card a five-year-old would give his *moooommy*. The words have to sound more grown-up."

"You're not very helpful and I'm running out of time."

"Sorry."

"My dad buys blank cards," Atul said, "and writes his own words to my mom."

"Good for him," Dexter muttered. He hated this. He grabbed a card and thrust it in Atul's face. "Read."

"That's more like it," Atul said, grinning. "A man with taste. I bet you picked a cool card for your aunt."

"What do you mean? She's not my mom and she never had kids."

"She's good to you. Get an aunt card then."

Dexter shrugged and quickly searched. "None."

"So get her a mother card. Doesn't she treat you like a son?"

I guess, Dexter thought, unwilling to take the notion further. Without replying to Atul, he searched the remaining cards, selected one, and showed it to him.

"Good one, I approve," Atul said.

Dexter elbowed his friend. "Like I need your approval. Spare me."

Atul just laughed. Dexter arrived home before Aunt Nicole. She was still at the hair salon. He added a spoonful of sugar to the lukewarm water, like he had seen Aunt Nicole do, and arranged the flowers in the simple glass vase he had purchased, thanks to more persuasion by Atul. Good thing Pacific Mall had been closing then, or he might have also brought home a husband for Aunt Nicole! And then he'd end up with a new dad to shop for on Father's Day next month. He banished those thoughts to another planet.

Aunt Nicole arrived home.

"You look lovely. These are for you," he offered.

"Thanks, Dexter." Surprised, she kissed him on the head and admired the mixed bouquet. "You must have smashed your piggy bank."

"I ... er ... don't have a piggy bank."

"I know. I'm just joking." She grinned.

Wow. How did I miss that? Dexter thought. *I'm getting too serious, like Mrs. Dhillon said.*

That night, as Dexter lay in bed, he thought of Aunt Nicole and everything she had done for him. Calling her "Aunt Nicole" seemed formal. "What shall I call her?" he mused aloud. She was now his second mom. "Mom II? Momsie? Mom Nicole?" His original mother was "Mom," so ... Suddenly, he was too tired to decide.

Next morning Dexter was up early. Nowhere near as early as on weekdays, but still early. Sunday was normally sleep-in time for both him and Aunt Nicole, and most Sundays they went to St. Aidan's Catholic Church on Finch for noon mass. But today was Mother's Day, so Dexter decided to brew a pot of her favourite tea combination — hibiscus and rosehips. He timed her exit from her bedroom and poured her a mugful.

"Happy Mother's Day, Aunt Nicole," he said, kissing her cheek and handing her the card. He watched her, knowing she would soon see what he'd written: "You are my mom now. I love you. Dexter."

She looked at him, tears falling down her cheeks. "Thank you," she said, then pulled him close for a hug. "I love you, too."

When at last she pulled away, she said, "Let's go out to brunch. Your choice."

"It's *your* day . . . Mom. Let's go to the Victorious Vegetarian Bistro. I know it's your favourite place."

Dexter watched as fresh tears sprang to her eyes.

12 A NEW IDEA

Dexter met with Coach Wilkinson in his office during lunch on Tuesday.

"I wanted to have a chat before today's match," Coach Wilkinson said.

What now? "I'm ready, Coach."

"I know you are, physically. Mental strategy is important also, as you well know. How're you getting along with the squad?"

"Fine."

Except for Boyd. Still can't figure out his problem. Maybe he's a middle child. I've heard the middle child can be the most confused in a family. Lucky, I'm the first and last rolled into one.

"Boyd suggested trying you at number four or the top of the middle order, number five."

That means I could end up partnering with Boyd if he keeps number three and the openers are dismissed. Wonder why he'd do that? Oh well, don't look a gift horse in the mouth, as my dad used to say.

"Personally I like the way you shone at number

seven last week," Coach Wilkinson added.

At that position, I get to observe the bowlers longer before batting.

"Hey, Coach, I'm flexible. Put me at number four today."

"Good to be flexible, Dexter."

"And who will be number seven?"

"Boyd. He wanted to try that out — mix things up a bit."

Ah, that explains it, thought Dexter. *Let the match begin.*

★★★

In the city's west end, Boyd lost the coin toss to the Exciters, who chose to bat second. In the squad briefing, Coach Wilkinson had said that the Exciters like to come from behind and surprise their opponents.

The Communicators' openers, Prakash and Sifiso, were dismissed by the Exciters with only six runs between them. Not a promising start. Cecil, who often was number four, had been pushed up to number three today. His batting, Dexter learned, could be up or down. One week hitting a respectable twenty-two, the next week a pitiful two. What kind of partnership would it be today?

Dexter started with a single and then got three sixes and a four before the over was, well, over. The Exciters changed their bowler fast before any more damage was done. The next bowler kept Dexter to singles, while dismissing number three and number four respectively, Cecil and Sugith. Partnering now with Ian, number six, Dexter was caught out by a high ball that the wind refused to carry over the boundary. He still got the highest score at 32, or as cricketers would say, he topscored 32.

Boyd replaced Dexter, nodding to him coldly as they passed each other.

You want to show off? Dexter thought. *Top that, Captain.*

Dexter was welcomed into the tent with high-fives. It was up to Boyd and the tailers. A miracle was needed. Boyd batted like a madman, like he was swatting away flies. Big flies. He hit a mixture of ones, twos, threes, his famous fours, and a six that almost caused him to fall backwards onto his wicket. The Communicators, tent-side, went wild cheering him on. He was run out, more through miscommunication with his partner, Ian, than fatigue. He showed why he was the captain by equalling Dexter's 32. Atul, Carlos, Benny, and Dan added a few runs each to the final, incredible season high of 81 runs.

"Excellent, guys, enjoy the feeling," said Coach. "Time to focus on your strength — defending. Protect your lead. Limit their scores as best you can. Remember some of the things that worked against the Stumpers last week. Hold them off. I believe you can do it." Coach Wilkinson held out his hand. The squad followed suit, Boyd still avoiding Dexter's hand.

"Communicators!" they all yelled.

Atul led off the bowling, easily dismissing the Exciters' openers, taking two wickets. Their upper order racked up 25 between them, as the Communicators' fielders lost focus and energy. Boyd got fired up. He moved them around the inner circle of the field to keep them alert and support the bowling efforts of Atul, Carlos, and Benny. That proved to be helpful in returning balls faster to wicket-keeper Dan, who stumped and ran out the upper order. The Exciters' middle order began to close the gap, scoring an additional 30. Atul took three wickets in succession, a hat trick, with his masterful yorkers, putting further pressure on the hosts. The Exciters, who previously responded well to challenges, fizzled. The final score was Communicators 81, Exciters 63.

For the Communicators, it was their widest margin of victory ever. They had sent a message that they were a formidable opponent to be reckoned with as the playoffs loomed. Their pre-playoffs season record was 4 wins, 3 losses, and 1 draw. Not bad!

★★★

That evening Dexter, Atul, and Sonia coordinated their battle plan to post the flyers without anyone seeing them. Dexter felt that it would be another step towards breaking down Principal Gagnon's resolve.

Early the next morning Dexter, Atul, Sonia, and

Mumbi (whom Sonia recruited), armed with masking tape and push pins, posted flyers on hallway corners and notice boards in every department. Dexter slipped one under Principal Gagnon's door. Sonia and Mumbi posted in all the female washrooms, staff included.

CRICKET
Suffolk Road Communicators
quieted
Wilson Avenue Exciters
★

Playoffs Next Week

Once again the morning announcement praised the Communicators' success. When Dexter went to his locker before lunch, he found one of the flyers stuck onto his locker with chewing gum and defaced with a big X drawn in black marker. He had not seen who placed it there. His best guess would be a baseball player. Any one of them. He didn't care.

***

The West Indies, a squad representing all the Caribbean islands plus Guyana, were playing a test match against India. Live. According to Atul, test matches were the most important matches in the sport. Three were played over the course of three days, and all three were held in the same place — the home of one of the squads.

"India and the West Indies — the Windies — have played many test matches over the years. Windies have won more than thirty times, India about twenty-four. And between them . . . are you ready for this?"

"Yes, Professor," said Dexter.

"Over forty draws between them," Atul declared.

"That sounds like the umpires saying, 'Call it a draw, fellas. Time to party.'"

"No, man, professional cricket is serious business. Careers at stake every step of the way." Atul continued his lecture. "India has been very strong since winning the last World Cup. But the Windies are on the rise once more, showing what the announcers call promise and flair."

The Dhillon household had settled into the spacious living room in front of the giant flat-screen TV to watch the game, being played at the Queen's Park Oval in Port-of-Spain, Trinidad. Would India decimate their hosts?

The boisterous spectators: Atul, Sonia, Mr. and Mrs. Dhillon, brother Saeed, sister Nita, Uncle Danny, neighbour Austin, Dexter, and Aunt Nicole.

On the side tables was the feast, catered by Uncle Danny Dhillon's restaurant, for continuous eating. The food: roti of course, as well as an amazing array of curries, both meat and vegetable; and half a dozen different sweets, including Dexter's favourite, *ladoo* — sweet yellow balls containing sugar, almonds, raisins, and cardamom.

Aunt Nicole had contributed some bottles of *mauby*, a drink made from the bark of a West Indian tree.

Once or twice Dexter noticed that Danny Dhillon, not a bad-looking guy for someone at least as old as his aunt, and single, seemed to pay a lot of attention to her. He wasn't sure how he felt about that.

Focusing again on the TV, Dexter saw an undulating sea of flag-waving, chanting spectators. The Windies had won the first match, India the second. Whoever won this match captured the First Test. Dexter watched a West Indian batsman score a "century" plus two runs (102), which took over three hours.

Then his eyes opened wide as the next batsman did something he had only ever seen in baseball. A skill he, Dexter Armstrong, the ambidextrous son of an ambidextrous man, had used in baseball — switch-hitting.

An idea bubbled while Dexter watched the batter switch from right side to left side at the popping crease, making single runs and fours and seeming to confound the bowler. The Indian bowler, who must have confronted this batter throughout the series and surely before — this was international cricket, after all — adjusted his delivery with determination. The batter was finally "clean bowled," that is, out. Middle stumps bent, bails floating upwards almost in slow motion, India erupted in cheers and congratulated the bowler. Yet the match was far from over.

Dexter turned to Atul beside him and they had a mind meld.

"You think it's possible?" Dexter asked.

"If you're brave enough," Atul replied.

The match came to a draw, and so, with each squad having a win and now a tie, the first Test series was "levelled." Dexter looked forward to watching the other Tests at the Dhillons' in the weeks ahead.

★★★

The following morning, before anyone else got there, Dexter and Atul practiced in the nets with Atul bowling slow balls. Dexter was developing a rhythm with his left-handed stroke. When Boyd entered the gym, Atul signalled and Dexter switched to his right side and batted. They had agreed that no one would see him switch-bat until he was comfortable.

"Dexter," Boyd said, "Coach and I agreed, you're back to number seven."

Dexter saw the position as an advantage. If Boyd was out before him, he wouldn't have to partner with him.

"Fine with me," said Dexter, continuing to bat.

"Why don't you guys play against the school wall or something?" Boyd said with a sneer.

"Aye aye, Capitano," said Atul sarcastically.

Dexter said nothing, just stared at Boyd. *Not the time, not the place,* he thought.

"Let's go, Atul," Dexter said, pulling him away.

13 PLAYOFFS

The grade seven and eight playoffs were played over three days. The Communicators had drawn Day Two, the Wednesday. Each school, by random selection, played two other schools. They were scheduled to play the Googlies and the Runners.

In the minibus, Coach Wilkinson was giving the Communicators a reminder of the strengths and weaknesses of the Googlies.

"Having said all of that, you need to be prepared because nothing is guaranteed," said Coach Wilkinson.

"Yes, men, we must be prepared like clansmen charging across the foggy marsh at dawn," Atul said with a pretty good Scottish accent.

Everyone cracked up,

"Get serious, guys," Boyd said after a moment. "I don't plan to be captain of a losing squad," said Boyd. "We lost last year and I don't want to do it again. Let's give Coach our attention."

They quieted down and looked at Coach Wilkinson, who was scratching his head.

"It's good to release your nervous energy through laughter," he said. "Better than keeping it bottled up. It can also clear your head so you can think better. And like I always say . . ."

"Have fun," they all chorused.

"All right," Coach said, "we'll be at the grounds soon. I want to go over the playoffs scoring one more time. The top eight squads, the ones with the most points, go through to Tournament Day next Thursday. Win or lose. No draws. A win is five points. A loss under five runs is three points. A loss by six to fifteen runs is two points. And a loss by sixteen or more runs is one point."

"Our aim is two wins, Communicators!" Boyd declared.

They all cheered, no one more loudly than Dexter.

★★★

The cheering section was smaller than it had been recently. Aunt Nicole could not get there for noon but promised to arrive in time for the second match. Mrs. Dhillon had properties to show all afternoon. Sonia had a presentation. Mumbi had told Sonia that she was busy catching up with assignments. Some parents and grandparents of other squad-mates did show up.

The Googlies, batting first, had beaten the

Communicators weeks before. They entered the play-offs on a two-match losing streak. The Communicators fielded as best they could to limit them to 52 runs, eyeing an easy target of 53.

During the changeover break, Atul sidled up to Dexter.

"Are you gonna do it?"

"My left side's still not strong enough."

"Maybe the second match? Think about it, Dexter."

"Okay, we'll see."

Despite the agility of the Googlies' bowlers and fielders, Boyd managed to score 20. Cecil got 15 hard-earned runs. The Communicators looked to Dexter to at least close the gap, if not surpass the target outright.

He scored a disappointing 11. Still, there was hope. Surely the four tailers would get 8 easy runs between them for victory. Sadly, no. The Communicators lost by 6.

Before the squad's spirits sank too far, Coach Wilkinson gathered the guys for a pep talk.

"You did well defensively to hold them to 52 runs. A low score. They edged us."

"I'm sorry I let you guys down," Dexter offered.

"You played as a unit," Coach said. "It was tough for them also. The last time they beat us by twenty runs."

"We still lost!" Boyd declared angrily.

Dexter avoided Boyd's gaze. "I will remind you," Coach went on, "that you have two points. Focus on doing your best to win our next match against the Runners. We still have a good chance of making Tournament Day."

Dexter's spirits were boosted upon seeing Aunt Nicole strolling to their tent. He was glad she hadn't witnessed his low score.

They got ready for the match against the Runners. Boyd won the coin toss. The Communicators would bat first.

Boyd got 32 runs. Cecil 15. Dexter 34, all from his right side. Atul 10.

Simply put, the Runners did not know what hit them. The Communicators won by twenty-two.

After the high-fives and victory shouts died down, Coach Wilkinson said, "Three schools are left to play to-morrow morning. By the afternoon we'll have full results."

"I'm sure we'll make it through," said Boyd. "Two plus five. Seven points out of ten."

"It still has to be official. Many schools could win both of their matches. Depends on the combinations," said Coach Wilkinson soberly, before he herded them onto the minibus. In bed that night, Dexter felt good that he had done his best to help the squad triumph over the Runners. Still, it nagged him that he performed so weakly during the first match against the Googlies. If they did not make it through to Tournament Day, everyone would point to him — the baseball screw-up, and now the cricket screw-up. He pondered all this before sleep finally claimed him.

★★★

The morning announcements came and went. There was no mention of the cricket squad, only a second-in-a-row loss by the baseball team.

Dexter's head throbbed from the pressure of waiting for the cricket results during English class. He excused himself, stumbled to the washroom, and splashed his face with cold water. Then he purchased a bottle of orange juice from the vending machine and sipped it, calming himself before returning to class.

Moments before the buzzer signalled the start of lunch, the secretary announced over the PA system for the Communicators cricket squad to meet in Coach Wilkinson's office.

By the time Dexter and Atul got to Coach Wilkinson's office door, he was standing outside with the others. They stood silently in fear and anticipation. Coach's face revealed nothing as he gazed at a faxed message.

Finally he looked up. "We made it through to Tournament Day!"

The Communicators erupted in cheers. Dexter felt more relief than elation. He would not be blamed for a loss.

"Practice after school," Coach Wilkinson said with a big smile. "We have work to do."

"Who do we play in Round One?" asked Boyd.

"The Spinners," Coach Wilkinson replied.

The squad they had lost once to and drawn with a couple of weeks ago.

"Grab some lunch, you'll need the energy," Coach Wilkinson said.

They dispersed joyously. Halfway down the hall, Dexter told Atul to go ahead to the cafeteria. He doubled back to Coach Wilkinson's office, looking both ways down the hallway before closing the door behind him.

"Dexter, I know you're eager to practice, but unfortunately I can't write a note to get you out of afternoon classes," Coach Wilkinson said. Dexter knew he was kidding.

"How much does a cricket ball cost, Coach?"

"About fourteen bucks."

"And a bat?"

"Roughly one hundred bucks."

"And to build a permanent cricket pitch?"

"Whoa! You won the lottery two minutes ago?"

"Seriously, Coach."

"Depending on the type of astro turf, around six thousand . . . Why?"

"Ms. Gagnon said that she's turned you down every year. She doesn't believe there's enough interest in cricket to spend on a pitch. But we've made it through playoffs. Let's go see her now."

"I've already dismissed the squad."

"No. Just you and me. I want to do this." Dexter

paused. "You won't get into trouble. I'll take full responsibility."

Coach Wilkinson chuckled. "Tell me your plan, Dexter Mastermind Armstrong."

★★★

The principal scribbled on a writing pad. "What you're saying, Dexter, is you want me to put up half the costs and you, coordinating the squad, will fundraise for the other half," she said.

Dexter nodded. "And Coach Wilkinson did not curse . . . cous . . ."

"Coerce," said Ms. Gagnon and Coach Wilkinson together.

"Co-erce me into any of this. It's all my idea."

The principal remained silent for a time. Then she met Dexter's gaze.

"Dexter, I am pleased with your progress on the cricket squad and how well you've kept your temper in check," she said. "But my answer is still no. I can't see you raising that kind of money with five weeks left in the school year."

Dexter released a long breath. "Thanks for seeing us, Ms. Gagnon."

Once outside the office, Coach Wilkinson turned to Dexter. "Sorry. I thought you had her. Thanks for your efforts, Dexter."

"I won't give up, Coach." And with that Dexter bolted towards the cafeteria in search of food.

★★★

When Dexter arrived home, exhausted from practice, Aunt Nicole presented him with an embossed t-shirt.

Brian Lara
400 Not Out

She also gave him a large book on cricket with many photographs.

His mouth fell open in surprise. Then he said, "Thanks, Mom," and gave her a huge hug.

He knew from Atul that Brian Lara, nicknamed The Prince, was an international batsman from Trinidad and Tobago who held the world record for the highest individual score in a Test Match — 400 runs, or quadruple century — ending with him being not out. This was back in 2004 against England. Having topscored 34, Dexter imagined a t-shirt with *Dexter Armstrong. 40 Not Out.*

"I'm taking next Thursday as a sick day," she announced. "I'll be at your tournament the entire day."

"That's great, Mom." And he meant every word.

★★★

Two days later Dexter decided to skip lunch and work on an assignment that was due the following week. With Tournament Day ahead, he did not want to fall behind with his school work. Entering the library, he spotted Mumbi seated at a table. He stood frozen, trying to decide whether to approach her. Just then, she looked up from her work and waved to him. He waved back. She gestured for him to join her. Dexter made his way towards Mumbi, glad that he was not sweaty like the last time they had a non-conversation in the gym.

"Hi, Dexter," she said, clearing some space on the table.

"Hi, Mumbi," he whispered, sitting opposite to her.

"Sorry I couldn't make it to Atul's to watch the cricket match," she said next.

"You like cricket?" he whispered again.

She rolled her eyes. "Yeah, of course! What's with the whispering? That's so twentieth-century-library."

"I didn't think you liked cricket," he said, speaking normally.

"Can't make assumptions about a girl you don't know, Dexter."

"I didn't mean to offend you," he said apologetically.

"I'm not offended. I don't offend easily."

Geez, she's tough, he thought. *To be a gymnast, you must be tough inside and out. I hope she's not a middle child.*

"I love cricket!" she blurted out. "I was on our grade six co-ed squad back in Vancouver. No girls play at this school, I found out."

"From cricket to gymnastics?"

"Gymnastics came first. Very disciplined." She groaned. "I started cricket for fun. I've been brushing up on gymnastics to assist at a beginners' camp this summer. What are you doing this summer?"

"If you're inviting me to go to gymnastics camp with you," he deadpanned, "I'll have to think about it. I've been known to stumble down the cricket pitch, not tumble."

Mumbi burst out laughing, and the librarian, Mrs. Gilliam, called out, "Quiet, you two."

"You're getting us in trouble," Mumbi said.

"She must be from the twentieth century."

Mumbi laughed even louder.

"Either you stay and work quietly or leave," Mrs. Gilliam said. "Which is it?"

They settled down to work, until Mrs. Gilliam took a phone call.

"I'm inviting you to Tournament Day," Dexter said in a low voice.

"Any girls playing from other schools?" she asked.

"No, all boys," he replied. "Vradenburg hosted an all-girls tournament last week already."

"Lemme think about it," she whispered back.

Mrs. Gilliam hung up the phone and glanced their way. They continued working for the rest of the lunch period, occasionally peeking at each other in smiling silence.

I survived that one! Dexter mused. *Hope she comes to the tournament.*

***

That afternoon Dexter and Atul lagged behind the squad during the warm-up jog.

"You're pretty brave asking a girl to take a *whole* day off school to see you hit some balls," Atul said.

"Like you wouldn't do the same," Dexter volleyed back.

"I haven't asked Sonia yet."

"What are you waiting for, never-ever-shy guy?"

"I'm getting some kind of attitude from her today."

"You'd better fix that. No Sonia, probably no Mumbi."

"Yes, Master. I keep forgetting you're so not inter-ested in Mumbi."

"It's cricket . . . not a date."

Coach Wilkinson blew his whistle and gathered them together. Today's practice would be a fun six-a-side match between the squad. Shirt tails out versus shirts tucked in.

Coach Wilkinson divided them with Dexter and Boyd on opposite sides.

14 SECRET PRACTICE

Dexter and Atul spent a lot of the weekend doing the same as they'd done over the past seven weeks since Dexter decided to learn cricket. They practiced the skills they would each need to be at their best on Tournament Day.

There was one thing different from the other weekends. It was the second anniversary of Dexter's parents' death. Alone in their car, they had died on impact. The drunk driver had survived, along with her toddler, who was in the back seat. Dexter never thought about the driver. Whenever he thought about the loss, he would feel tense and not know why. He would focus on something else: school work or listening to steel pan music, traditional Trinidad and Tobago music he'd always loved. Dexter's parents had been cremated. He and Aunt Nicole had scattered their ashes at the base of Scarborough Bluffs into Lake Ontario. The Bluffs had been a place his parents loved to go.

Aunt Nicole had arranged a memorial mass for Saturday afternoon. He did not share this with Atul, just practiced his switch batting and pedalled home when he and Atul were done. He wasn't looking forward to this mass.

Dexter and Aunt Nicole drove to St. Aidan's. Dexter felt tears well up in his eyes as the priest said, "This mass is being said for the repose of the souls of Nellie Armstrong and Eugene Armstrong. May they rest in peace." His aunt was teary-eyed, too, and she kept clutching his hand. He just wanted this to be over. He didn't need the reminder that his parents were no longer around, would never be around again.

And yet . . . that night, Dexter dreamed of his parents strolling hand-in-hand through the grassy field that overlooked the Bluffs. They seemed at peace.

★★★

On Monday morning Dexter, Atul, Sonia, and Mumbi swung into action once more. Although there had been a PA announcement Friday about the Communicators' success, they posted even more flyers around the school this time. After all, it was Finals. Dexter felt that if most of the school was encouraged to come out for Baseball Finals or Track and Field Finals, why not cricket?

CRICKET
Suffolk Road Communicators
Advance to Tournament Day
Thursday, June 1, 9–3:30
Sunnybrook Park Cricket Grounds
All Welcome!

The flyers created a buzz about cricket throughout the school. Students actually showing up might be another matter.

The principal paid a visit to Coach Wilkinson and the squad just before practice that afternoon.

"Hello, guys," Ms. Gagnon began. "I wanted to take a moment to wish you the best of luck as you represent Suffolk Road on Tournament Day. School Board business will prevent me from being there. I have also come to make you an offer. I have been charmingly pestered by Dexter Armstrong to build a permanent pitch here on this field."

The squad murmured among themselves.

"Also, Coach Wilkinson before him," she continued. "If you make it to the final round on Thursday, I will pay for half of the costs to build the pitch. You will fundraise for the other half."

Cheers rose from the squad. Principal Gagnon raised her hands to quiet them.

"Should you win the championship . . . I will find a way to cover the entire cost."

The squad cheered as if they had already won.

"Ms. Gagnon, speaking for the squad, we thank you for your offer and graciously accept your terms," Coach Wilkinson beamed.

Ms. Gagnon smiled at Coach Wilkinson and gave Dexter a wink that he interpreted as, *Your move next.*

"*Bonne chance,*" she said to all, and headed back to the school building.

Coach Wilkinson started the practice. "Today we will work on fielding situations," he announced. "Take your positions."

They started to disperse. Boyd brushed past Dexter. "Perhaps *you* should be made captain. It's not too late."

Puzzled, Dexter looked at him and then walked to his *square leg* position, left of the batter.

Coach Wilkinson removed a bat from the kit bag and handed it to Sifiso. "You will bat first. I want you to place the ball in every possible direction. Keep the fielders guessing where the ball might end up. Benny, you will bowl slow easy ones. Boyd, move your fielders as you think is appropriate. I'll stop things from time to time."

During the drill, Boyd repeatedly moved Dexter from position to position, often changing his mind and confusing him. Dexter looked at Coach Wilkinson, but he did not seem to notice Boyd's subtle directions.

The practice came to a close. Dexter and Atul began to dismantle the wickets. Coach Wilkinson rolled up the pitch mat with help from Benny, Carlos, and Ian. Boyd supervised the collection of cones and discs from around the field. Coach Wilkinson, Benny, Carlos, and Ian started wheeling the mat towards the school building. Dexter was alone for a moment packing up the kit case.

Boyd approached him. "Think you're good enough to be captain, don't you? Getting on Coach's side?" Dexter knew it was a taunt and not a sincere question. When he did not respond, Boyd pressed further, "I heard your parents ran away to the Caribbean without their *baggage*." He gave Dexter a shove. "That's you, orphan boy," he sneered.

Dexter stumbled, recovered, and shoved Boyd back, causing him to fall onto his back. Dexter balled his fist and towered over Boyd. At that moment, Dexter heard Coach Wilkinson shout, "Stop that!"

He ran over. "Dexter, have you lost your mind? You know I won't tolerate this kind of behaviour!"

Dexter was mortified. He hadn't been actually going to hit Boyd, just scare him enough to stop the nasty words. "Coach, I —"

"You looked me in the eye and promised that you would not let me down," Coach said. "Well, you have. And you have let down the integrity of this squad. It's *not* cricket!"

Atul tried to speak up in Dexter's defence. "It's not how —"

"Turn your things in right now, Dexter. You're suspended!" Coach stormed off.

Dan called out, "But, Coach, Dexter could help us win."

Coach Wilkinson turned back, addressing the squad. "How many times do I have to say that this isn't about winning? It's about building your character for everything you will ever do. Good to win in the course of it, yes. Would you rather win as hooligans? Thugs?" Coach Wilkinson headed towards the school building.

Dexter ran towards a different door. Atul called out to him but he didn't look back. In the change room, Dexter stripped off his uniform and put on his regular school clothes, then dropped off his uniform and fielding cap in front of Coach Wilkinson's door. He didn't bother to knock. Who cared if Coach was in his office? Not him.

He raced home. When Aunt Nicole saw him, she asked, "Is everything okay, Dexter?"

He nodded and headed to his room, refusing to talk. His phone rang but he ignored it. He did not want any pity from Atul or anyone else. After a while he went into the kitchen and made a batch of oatmeal and raisin muffins. The task didn't do much to soothe him, not the way it usually did. And eating one soothed his hunger, but not his anger.

Aunt Nicole simply gave him some space. When Dexter went to bed, sleep was a long time coming.

★★★

In the morning, Dexter woke up feeling like crap. He pondered whether he should stay at home or go to school and face everyone, especially the principal.

On the kitchen table was a note: "Dexter, honey, I don't know what you're dealing with, but trust your inner guidance to help you make the right decisions. Love, Mom."

Dexter arrived at school intent on making sure Coach Wilkinson heard his side of the story. He was locking his bike at the stand when the coach approached him.

"Good morning, Dexter. I'd like you to come with me. Please."

They walked in silence past the main office. Dexter was surprised that they did not go into Ms. Gagnon's office. They continued through the hallways to Coach Wilkinson's office. Dexter was preparing to blurt out his story first when he noticed Boyd seated inside. Coach Wilkinson closed the door, opened a folding chair, and offered Dexter a seat while he sat behind his desk.

"I wanted to speak to both of you together. Yesterday, as I was heading to my car, Dan, Sifiso, and Atul stopped me. They had seen everything." Coach Wilkinson looked at Dexter. "I have already had a chat with Boyd this morning and he has admitted his role in yesterday's incident, along with his taunting of you ever since you joined the squad."

Dexter glanced at Boyd, who shifted uneasily in his chair.

Coach Wilkinson continued, "Dexter, I am so sorry that I did not listen to your side of things. I apologize for my . . . bull-headed actions," he said. "I was wrong."

Dexter stared at him. He was about to speak, but was stopped by Boyd, who said, "Dexter . . . I'm sorry for my behaviour as a fellow cricketer and a captain. Will you accept my apology?" He extended his hand.

Dexter looked at Boyd's hand, nodded, and shook it without saying anything.

"Dexter, will you join our squad again?" Coach Wilkinson asked.

Dexter glanced at both of them. Boyd's shy smile was genuine. Here it was — a simple request. Heartfelt. Not because they wanted to win a championship. Another coach might have said, "Your suspension's lifted, see you at practice." This was different. He had worked so hard to be a part of this squad, never fully feeling like a member. In this moment, Dexter felt a measure of control over his destiny. He could say no and end the year seeing himself as a victim. Or . . .

Dexter wanted to play cricket now more than ever before. He wanted to win for his school and he wanted to have that permanent pitch built — for Coach Wilkinson and for the cricketers to follow. The boys and — he thought of Mumbi — someday, the girls.

"Yes!" he shouted, jumped up and high-fived Coach Wilkinson and Boyd, feeling new-found joy.

★★★

Atul joined Dexter briefly for lunch. He was happy to have his friend and squad-mate back to normal. He left Dexter saying that he had a relationship to save — with Sonia.

Boyd got up from a neighbouring table and approached Dexter. "I wanna talk to you some more, Dexter, but not here. Let's go outside, okay?"

Dexter downed the last of his juice. "Sure."

They started walking along the street.

"You nervous about Thursday?" Boyd asked.

"Not so much nervous as excited. I'll probably get nervous when the first ball comes barrelling down the pitch."

"Just don't close your eyes."

"Not a chance."

"When I first moved here from Australia last year, the captain used to tease me . . . 'cause of my accent . . . and 'cause I was an all-rounder, though stronger batting than bowling. He thought I wanted to be captain. I didn't."

"And you gave me a hard time because you thought *I* wanted to be captain."

"I'd only been captain a few weeks, mate. You were

this hotshot baseball player. You probably had a dozen personal cheerleaders carrying you around the field every time you hit a home run."

Dexter laughed.

Boyd chuckled. "Dexter, I knew about your city championship last year. And you started to hit the bat so, well, natural like. And then you — not me, the team captain — lobby the principal for a pitch. Thought for sure Coach'd make you captain."

"No way. Coach is no fool, you know. Don't you see how much he trusts your decisions?"

They turned into the schoolyard.

"Hadn't thought of it much. He's a good guy, Coach."

"Yep," Dexter said. "And you're a good captain, Boyd."

He meant it, too.

★★★

That evening Dexter thought about everything — his anger issues, his aunt, his parents, and Boyd's taunts, especially the one about his parents abandoning him like baggage. As strange as it sounded, he had felt like his parents had abandoned him, like they had left on a permanent vacation. He felt like luggage left behind. Stray, forgotten luggage his aunt was forced to pick up. For the first time, he realized that he didn't have to think that way. He knew that Aunt Nicole loved him. And his parents had loved him, too.

★★★

Dexter and Atul did their last twenty-minute session in secret. Dexter stood in the nets and batted from his left side while Atul bowled easy balls and spinners. Hits. Misses. Some awkward shots. Putting it all together would be the trick, alongside his right-handed batting. It would not be enough to surprise the bowlers. Dexter had to achieve a level of comfort as well.

"Time's up," Atul said. "Or our secret could be discovered."

Dexter switched to his right side. This part of their practice was for Atul to exercise his now-merciless fast-bowling skills. Dexter did not have to be accurate in playing the shots. That was how Coach Wilkinson found them that morning before they surrendered the nets to other squad-mates.

"Think I'm ready?" Dexter asked Atul.

"Practice is one thing. Whatever you decide, don't jeopardize the squad."

"I'll keep that in mind," Dexter said.

★★★

In the afternoon Coach Wilkinson joined the squad in

the field after their warm-up. His hands were behind his back.

"Where's the mat and kit cases, Coach?" asked Boyd.

The squad members looked at one another.

"Spread out," Coach Wilkinson instructed, bringing his hands in front of him to reveal a soccer ball.

For fifteen minutes the squad members tossed the ball to each other, calling the boy's name they were sending it to. As they continued, sometimes laughing, Coach Wilkinson quietly moved each player until they were in a small circle.

"And . . . stop," Coach Wilkinson said. "This ends your practice, guys. You're a unit. Get an early sleep. We meet here at seven-thirty tomorrow morning. Dismissed."

Nobody moved.

"That's it, Coach?" Dexter asked.

"That's it," Coach Wilkinson said with a warm smile.

15 TOURNAMENT DAY

Squad by colourful squad, eighty-eight grade seven and eight cricketers and their alternates strode through the ivy-garlanded archway onto Sunnybrook Park Cricket Grounds. Hallowed grounds on a high plateau overlooking the city of Toronto.

The nine o'clock sun in a blue, cloudless sky gave promise of a perfect day. Dexter was rested and pumped. Three months ago he could not have even imagined being a cricketer. And yet here he was, pleased and excited to be part of the squad.

Each squad, led by their coach or coaches, then their captain, assembled in a huge circle around Pitch #1, along with the umpires. In a wider arc covering half the cricket field's edge, the spectators — students, relatives, friends, guests — rose to their feet. Among them were Aunt Nicole, Mrs. Dhillon, Danny Dhillon, Sonia, and, yes, Mumbi. Dexter counted about thirty from Suffolk Road PS.

After "O Canada" was played over the loudspeaker,

Barry Lakti, a former Canadian national cricket captain, said a few words to the squads, concluding with, "... Be the sportsmen this day you have always aspired to be. Play with fairness, with character, and with passion. Above all, enjoy yourselves. And we will enjoy you. I now declare Tournament Day *open*."

The first four squads for Round Number One retired to their red pop-up tents, except for the captains, who remained for the coin toss. Boyd lost. The Spinners elected to field first. Eight overs. Six fair balls to be bowled each over. Fast matches.

Dexter introduced Mumbi to Aunt Nicole and to Danny Dhillon.

"I'm glad you came," Dexter said to Mumbi.

"Like I said, I love cricket," Mumbi smiled.

And you kinda like me or you wouldn't be here, he thought. *I like you, too.*

Sifiso and Prakash opened with a blistering 14 runs between them. Boyd lifted the score with 20. Dexter started batting with his right side. After a few warm-up singles, he switched to his left side. No one really noticed at first. He hit a double. Back to his right side, a single. Back to left side, a four. The Communicators' tent was a combination of jaw-dropping speechlessness and continuous cheering.

Boyd shook his head and called out, "You're full of surprises, Dexter. Keep it up, mate."

Coach Wilkinson scratched his head and turned to

Boyd, asking, "Did you know about this?"

"Not a clue, Coach," said Boyd.

"Neither did I," Coach Wilkinson muttered.

"Patience, Dexter," Atul called out.

The bowlers were unable to contain Dexter. Eventually he was caught out while attempting a six — though batting right side at the time — with 17 runs. He would not be accused of being reckless.

"Good job, Dexter," Coach Wilkinson patted him on the back.

Boyd high-fived him.

"That was brave, buddy. Where'd you learn those moves?" said Atul, grinning from head to toe.

With an all out 56 runs, the Spinners faced a target of 57. No draws today.

Atul led off the bowling. He took the first four wickets quickly, surprising the Spinners. On this day they were no match for the charging Communicators.

Round One to the Communicators, 56–48.

Meanwhile, on Pitch #2, the Flyers had barely edged the Stumpers.

The second half of Round Number One saw the defending champions, the Googlies, trounce the Breakers. The Trotters sneaked past the Exciters.

Dexter, Atul, Boyd, and Sifiso had watched the Googlies and the Breakers, knowing that they would face the winner next. The Googlies had beaten them by six runs in the playoffs.

***

Round Two. The Semi-Finals. The Communicators, batting first, scored a fast-paced 68 all out. Boyd, 27. Dexter, 24, also catching the Googlies' bowlers off guard with his switch-batting.

The Googlies were chasing 69. They were out-classed, outbowled, and outmatched mainly by one bowler — Atul, who took six wickets with a ferocity seldom seen at this level. Until . . .

Atul ran up towards the crease, adding his trademark hop to give him more mid-air delivery power. Reaching the crease, he tripped and crashed forward flat onto the pitch. He yelped in pain and grabbed his ankle.

Dexter and Coach Wilkinson rushed to him. Then a medic hurried over and determined that his ankle was not broken. They lifted Atul to his feet. He winced as he put his foot down. They carried him off the pitch to the tent, where Mrs. Dhillon attended to him.

Carlos and Benny completed the bowling, taking wickets. The match ended with a spectacular textbook catch by Boyd into his chest.

The chief umpire pointed his right forefinger high in the air. Out! 68–41.

The Googlies would regroup for the eight-overs consolation match against the Flyers or the Trotters on Pitch #2.

Under the Communicators' tent, there was concern

as well as rejoicing. Atul couldn't play, but he insisted on staying till the end.

"Okay, let's raise your leg a bit higher to get the swelling down," Mrs. Dhillon said, pressing an ice pack to his ankle.

Sonia brought Atul a box of juice. Then he clapped his hands and gestured for the Communicators to give him their attention. "It's all up to you guys now. I'll sit here and be entertained." There was an undercurrent of sadness to his speech. He was clearly Man of the Match, the player who'd performed with extraordinary skill against the Googlies, and his squad-mates let him know that.

Coach Wilkinson announced that Ryan would be the additional batsman with Boyd as the third bowler. Meanwhile, on Pitch #2, the Flyers had beaten the Trotters. Lunch was called.

Coach took Boyd aside for some practice bowling through most of the twenty-minute lunch break.

Aunt Nicole handed Dexter a sandwich along with a box of juice. Mumbi joined him on the grass with her lunch, saying, "I'm getting the itch to play again."

"Funny, I've been thinking of coaching a girls' squad," Dexter said.

"You have not. Liar."

"You don't think I could do it?"

"I think you could do whatever you set out to," she said quietly.

Her comment both thrilled and embarrassed Dexter. He took a big bite of his sandwich. Mumbi did the same with hers, and the pair of them finished their food in silence.

When Mumbi spoke again, she said, "Lie back on the grass, Dexter."

"Mumbi, you want to make out?"

"You wish!" she said and pushed him onto his back. "Close your eyes. I'll wake you in exactly five minutes."

Dexter obeyed, closing his eyes. He listened to the sounds of people calling to one other. Practice balls hitting bats. The smells of different foods wafting in the breeze. Mumbi's subtle lemony perfume. He felt the sun on his face and his body relaxed. And he wished that Mumbi would lean down and kiss him, like on television, as he floated off into . . .

"Time's up," she said.

"Where am I?" He opened his eyes and sat up. "Is the match over?"

Mumbi rolled her eyes. "Only *lunch* is over. Get out there. I'll be watching you," she said playfully.

Dexter got up, stretched, and strolled over towards the tent. He looked back. Mumbi was still looking at him with an encouraging smile.

So this is what having a girlfriend feels like, he thought It was a good feeling.

16 FINAL OF FINALS

Communicators versus Flyers. Ten overs. Sixty good balls each to be bowled.

Boyd won the coin toss and elected to field first. Carlos was the lead bowler. The Flyers' opening partnership quickly racked up 12 runs in the first over. By the sixth over, the Flyers had amassed 65. Boyd, as bowler, had taken two surprising wickets. Boyd moved the Communicators around the field in constant anticipation. Dexter looked towards their tent and saw Atul with his head in his hands.

Dexter bent down on one knee as the ball sped towards him. He scooped it up, turned, and zoomed it to wicket-keeper Dan, who caught it and broke the bails off, stumping the batter before he could reach the crease. *Out!*

The Flyers' tent was very vocal, boosting their squad-mates.

"Make the singles and doubles!" yelled the Flyers' coach. "I don't need any Sachin Tendulkars out there!"

Dexter knew from Atul that Tendulkar was considered one of the greatest batsmen of all time.

With singles and doubles, the Flyers increased to an astounding 86, setting a target of 87 for the Communicators to chase.

During the changeover break, Coach Wilkinson gathered the squad outside the tent. "Keep your focus," he said. "Look for weak spots in their fielding positions and place the ball there. Watch the ball carefully and don't chase the wides in desperation."

"They favour yorkers and sneak in about two bouncers each over," Atul offered.

"Good. Keep an eye out. Play them as best you can," Coach Wilkinson instructed. "It's been a long day. They're tired, too. Sip water and stay hydrated. Dexter, I'm switching you to number three, Boyd to number seven to give you more rest."

Dexter nodded, understanding the strategy. He was anxious to face the Flyers.

Sifiso and Prakash opened and scored a mere 8 between them before Sifiso was caught out. As Dexter was sent out to replace him, Boyd stopped him, advising, "Keep your head still so you can anticipate the bowlers better. I'm counting on you, Dexter. Go get 'em."

Dexter nodded and strode onto the field with his sword-like bat. *A gladiator.* Looking around, Dexter noted that the number of spectators was larger than for previous matches. Then he waved to Prakash, who waved back, establishing communication.

He instantly racked up 12 runs before Prakash was *run out*. Cecil and Sugith were bowled out instantly, sending stumps and bails flying. Dexter now began switch-batting, scoring 15 more to total 27. The Flyers' captain moved his fielders accordingly each time to anticipate where Dexter would place the ball. Each time, Dexter found their weakest spot.

Boyd joined Dexter. This partnership scored 25 between them. Boyd managed 15 before he was bowled out. Walking off, he whispered to Dexter, "Keep going, mate, you're doing well."

Dexter, having survived for over forty-five minutes, was near exhaustion, but Boyd's words gave him renewed strength.

The Flyers' coach was very vocal. "Don't let 'em catch up. Come on, Felix, get him out."

Through those comments, Dexter heard Atul loud and clear shouting, "Great batting, Dexter! Don't let them rattle you. Stay alive!"

Dexter faced a bouncer at chest level. He leaned back and pulled for another spectator-rousing six, giving him a personal high of 43. Dexter's hands tingled from all of the striking. He shook his hands out and glanced at the scoreboard. With the Communicators at 75, twelve more would give them victory. Last over. Six good balls left. Benny and Dan still to bat.

Benny was caught within seconds. Dan rushed out and hit a single. Dexter a double. Dan a double. Dexter a single. Six more runs to victory. Dexter heard something no batter liked to hear.

"Last ball," the head umpire called.

One ball. Hit a six — victory. Anything else — defeat.

"Go for it, Dexter!" Atul screamed.

Dexter stared down the bowler, who ran up and delivered a yorker right at Dexter's feet. Dexter had practiced this with Atul often enough to recognize it quickly. In baseball, it would be an unplayable low ball with no wicket to strike. But this was cricket, not baseball.

Dexter, the gladiator, hooked it with the toe of his bat. The ball sailed up, up, beyond, towards a spot no one covered nor could cover quickly enough. Dexter screamed at it.

"Go ... go ... go ... gooooo ..."

The spectators rose in unison.

On this sunny afternoon, there was no strong wind to lift this particular shot. And so it bounced, once, just inside the boundary, and hopped over the boundary for four.

So close!

The spectators went wild — for a variety of reasons, regardless who they were rooting for. They had been entertained. The Flyers rushed to each other in jubilation. The Communicators, visibly disappointed, knew that it was a victory of sorts for them. They consoled each other. They, too, had climbed a mountain, but were unable to plant the flag.

★★★

Closing Ceremony.

The squads lined up. With genuine, proper sportsmanship, the Communicators congratulated the Flyers who hoisted the Crystal Cup with well-earned pride. 86–85.

Dexter was presented with the Man of the Match trophy for his 50 runs — a half-century — a new Tournament Day record. He was cheered by all, including the Flyers. He had slammed them for 50, not out.

The Flyers each were awarded a round, red crest and a grade seven and eight Cricket Champions banner. The Communicators each received a round, blue crest and a grade seven and eight Cricket Finalists banner. They posed for squad photos.

Coach Wilkinson, with unabashed tears, said, "You're the best squad I have had the privilege to coach. I thank each of you for the commitment and dedication you have shown. Hold your heads high."

They applauded him, knowing what he had done for them individually and collectively as a unit.

Aunt Nicole screamed and hugged Dexter. He felt a little embarrassed as his squad-mates looked on. But he hugged her back. Mumbi gave him an excited high-five and their fingers entwined. It was their first real physical contact.

"Impressive, Dexter, my boy. You did good," Atul said.

"You, too," Dexter said, touching knuckles. "You were a beast in your last game."

"Good job, Dexter." Boyd high-fived him.

"You, too, Captain," Dexter replied.

Coach Wilkinson approached Dexter away from everyone. "I'm glad I chose you, Dexter. You've made me proud. Thank you."

"Don't thank me yet, Coach," he said deflecting the compliment. "You can't coach a new squad with only half a pitch, they'll laugh at you. We've got money to raise, people to beg from, chocolates to push on neighbourhood children, politicians to petition, and wealthy teachers to solicit. Work to do, work to do."

Coach Wilkinson laughed and slapped Dexter on the back.

17 FINAL OFFERS

Aunt Nicole woke Dexter before she left for work. He sat up in bed.

"Dexter, I was wondering if you still wanted to go to baseball camp this summer."

"I forgot all about that," he said around a yawn.

"I took that part-time job so that you could go. I stopped when I had enough put aside. I was going to surprise you."

"Wow! I'm sorry, Aun— Mom. I don't need baseball camp anymore. Take a nice vacation with the money. You could use it."

"Is it that obvious?" she asked looking at her face in the mirror. "Here's an idea I'd like you to think over. I could take you to see your grandfather in Trinidad for six weeks." She grinned.

His eyes widened. "See Grandpa? Wow! Fresh coconut water for breakfast every morning and not from a can?"

"I can arrange it."

"Is Danny Dhillon coming, too?"

Aunt Nicole was taken aback. "Danny? You've been observant. We're taking things slowly. Tell me, truthfully, how would you feel if he did go with us?"

"Fine. It's good for you to have a steady-steady."

"That's what you guys call it? In Trinidad we say 'every bread have a cheese.'" She looked at her watch. "Time for me to go."

"If I accept your offer," Dexter said, "can we come back in time for the CNE?"

The Canadian National Exhibition was one thing about Toronto Dexter looked forward to every year.

Aunt Nicole giggled. "Can't miss the Ex. All right, son."

***

When Dexter arrived in homeroom, Atul was there with his ankle bandaged and a pair of crutches near his desk.

"Holy . . . !" Dexter exclaimed.

"I had x-rays. Nothing broken. Just a sprain. My choices were either use crutches and promise to keep off my foot as much as possible, or no crutches and stay at home for a week of pampering from Mrs. Dhillon."

"Good choice. Atul, I want to thank you for teaching me cricket. And for making this an exciting end to grade eight for me," Dexter said solemnly.

"You're welcome. Was fun to have my buddy along." He paused. "Hey, did you practice that speech in front of a mirror?" he joked.

Students started to pour in. Dexter took his seat, not bothering to answer Atul.

So what if he can't take a compliment? Like I can?

The nine o'clock bell sounded. The principal came over the PA system asking the entire school to file down to the gym for a special assembly.

Dexter and Atul looked at each other and shrugged.

Along the way, all of the cricket squad were intercepted and directed onto the stage. On stage sat Coach Wilkinson, Ms. Gagnon, and Mrs. Goldstein, Superintendent of Education for their area schools. The principal welcomed everyone, saying how proud she was of the Communicators' efforts. And then she mentioned the offer she had made.

"The grade seven and eight Communicators Cricket Squad came within two runs of victory — the best result ever for our school. In my mind, as ambassadors for our school, you are all victorious," she said, to loud applause and turned the podium over to Mrs. Goldstein.

"Congratulations Communicators and Coach Wilkinson. I am here to say that you won't have to raise the other half of the costs for your permanent pitch — I'll be matching Ms. Gagnon's offer," Mrs. Goldstein announced.

The squad cheered to thunderous applause and watched as the blue grade seven and eight Cricket Finalist banner was raised in the gym alongside banners from other sports teams.

★★★

After school Dexter and Mumbi strolled through Terry Fox Park, enjoying each other's company and munching on *dan tas*.

"A summer in Trinidad? You're lucky," said Mumbi.

"I guess. Yes, I am lucky. I'll be with family."

"Sonia invited me to the Dhillons' on Sunday," Mumbi said. "For the second India–Windies Test Series."

"And what did you tell her?"

"I said that it was a nice offer, but I'll only go if Dexter Armstrong will be there."

"And will Dexter Armstrong be there?"

"He'd better be," she said, playfully shoving him.

BE A PRO!
KNOW THE LINGO

all-rounder: A player who is skilled at both batting and bowling.

all out: A side is all out when ten of the eleven batters are dismissed or retired.

boundary: The edge of the cricket field marked by a rope or cones. If the ball is hit and crosses the rope/cones, the batter scores four runs. Six runs are scored if it hasn't bounced before crossing the rope/cones.

clean bowled: When a batter completely misses the ball and is bowled out by delivery.

crease: The areas around the stumps marked with white lines.

extras: Runs that are not scored by the batter: wides, no-balls, byes, and leg byes.

hat trick: When a bowler takes three wickets in successive deliveries — not necessarily in a single over.

Howzat?: "How is that?" A shout made in appeal to the umpire.

innings: The period in which one squad bats.

nets: A practice area surrounded by netting where batters and bowlers can develop their skills in a confined area.

openers: The two batters who bat first for a squad.

over: A division of play — six *good* successive deliveries bowled by the same bowler to the batter. Wide or unplayable balls do not count.

off-spin bowler: A right-handed bowler who spins the ball using the fingers, making it move from left to right when it lands.

partnership: The runs scored by two batters batting together.

pull shot: A type of shot played by swinging the bat in front of the body and hitting the ball to the *leg* side.

run: A unit of scoring. It is credited to the batting squad if the striker and non-striker run to the opposite ends of the pitch without being run out or caught.

run out: When a batter's wicket is broken with the ball as they are attempting a run.

spin bowling: A type of bowling where the bowler adds spin to the ball with the fingers or wrist to make it turn or deviate sideways when it lands.

stump: Three vertical poles of wood (stumps) and two short bails (wooden cylinders) balanced over the stumps make up the wicket. The wicket-keeper can "stump" a batter by breaking the wicket when the batter is out of their crease.

test match: The highest form of cricket, with national

teams playing matches for two innings each for a maximum of five days' play.

toe: The very bottom edge of a bat.

wicket: The arrangement of stumps and balls at each end of the pitch.

yorker: A delivery pitched on or around the popping crease and aimed to slide under the bat, catching the batter by surprise.

ACKNOWLEDGEMENTS

I wish to thank my editors, Carrie Gleason and Maryan Gibson, for their insightful clarity and dedication to the manuscript. And the Lorimer team — the process was smooth and fun-filled. Special thanks goes to Tim Stone of Vradenburg PS for his kindness and expertise in cricket at the elementary school level, as well as his nurturing of both boys' and girls' cricket. Thanks also to Peter Raymond for advice and introducing me to Tim. My gratitude goes to Umberto Cataudella, Lu Cormier, Angela Macri, Eileen Nemzer, and Ainajugoh Taylor for their heartfelt support.